"There was
of whom y

Jared spoke with deceptive softness.

Kris was shaking inside, hurt and mindlessly angry. Not *him*? Jared Chayse and Kris Laurensen. Together, their individual fortunes would cement a financial empire, thus preserving it for a further generation. The logistics of such a union were abundantly clear.

"The possibility must surely have occurred to you?" he drawled, and her pulse seemed to leap and throb into frantic life.

"Would you believe no? But naturally I'm expected to see the wisdom of your proposal!" she essayed cynically. The thought of becoming Jared's wife, sharing his bed, needed careful consideration. Part of her wanted to refuse, *now*. Yet there was a wild reckless streak urging acceptance, daring her to be swept into an emotional vortex and be damned to the consequences.

HELEN BIANCHIN, originally from New Zealand, met the man she would marry in Australia on a tobacco farm. Danilo, an Italian immigrant, spoke little English. Helen's Italian was nil. But communicate they did, and within eight weeks, Danilo found the words to ask Helen to marry him. With such romantic beginnings, it's a wonder that the author waited until after the birth of their third child to begin her prolific romance-writing career.

Books by Helen Bianchin

HARLEQUIN PRESENTS

HARLEQUIN ROMANCE

Don't miss any of our special offers. Write to us at the following address for information on our newest releases.

Harlequin Reader Service
901 Fuhrmann Blvd., P.O. Box 1397, Buffalo, NY 14240
Canadian address: P.O. Box 603,
Fort Erie, Ont. L2A 5X3

HELEN BIANCHIN

dark enchantment

Harlequin Books

TORONTO • NEW YORK • LONDON
AMSTERDAM • PARIS • SYDNEY • HAMBURG
STOCKHOLM • ATHENS • TOKYO • MILAN

Harlequin Presents first edition May 1987
ISBN 0-373-10975-X

Original hardcover edition published in 1986
by Mills & Boon Limited

CHAPTER ONE

THE giant Boeing banked slightly in preparation for its cruising descent, allowing Kris a brief glimpse of Sydney's sprawling metropolis beneath its silver wing, revealing the Opera House as a priceless sculpture set against a turquoise blue sea.

After a year spent abroad it felt immeasurably good to be returning home, and she endured the mechanics of disembarkation and Customs with familiar ease. On emerging into the arrival lounge she was greeted by a man of middle years whose uniformed, peak-capped presence garnered speculative interest of a kind Kris had become accustomed to dealing with from an early age.

'The car's right outside,' he informed her briskly, taking care of the luggage trolley, and an impish sparkle lit her eyes.

'In a no-parking zone, Sam? One of these days you'll get booked.'

'Only if some rookie becomes over-zealous in the line of duty,' he returned easily. 'Besides, the Laurensen number-plates carry sufficient weight to——'

'Ensure those in authority turn a blind eye,' Kris finished dryly as she preceded him through the self-opening doors to the elegant white Rolls Silver Spirit parked against the kerb.

Angela Laurensen gloried in projecting an image of extreme wealth, Kris reflected as she slipped into the rear seat. If perchance Sam was not available with the Rolls, then her dear stepmama showed not the slightest qualm in hiring a chauffeured limousine for the day—another Rolls, of course, for a lesser car would be impossible to endure.

'Anything of importance happen while I was away, Sam?' Kris enquired idly as the luxurious vehicle glided regally through traffic intent on vacating the busy international terminal.

'You want a run-down on the state of the Australian economy?' he queried, easing on to the main road. 'The price of fuel, share indices—that sort of thing?'

He was deliberately teasing her, and Kris wrinkled her nose at him in silent admonition as she caught his amused gaze in the rear-vision mirror.

Sam and Suzy Pemberton had been employed in the Laurensen household for as long as Kris could remember. Long before her father had married the glamorous Angela.

'Angela's cordially written missives tend to be filled with as mattering of gossip, parties, dinners given and attended. A quarterly report on the state of Chayse-Laurensen's financial affairs is despatched via Jared and accompanied by a few personally penned words. All told, it makes for stimulating reading,' she concluded with a faint grimace, unable to dispel a faint feeling of unease.

Was it unreasonable to expect some perspective regarding her future? Surely at twenty—almost twenty-one, she corrected silently—her education was complete. It wasn't that she was ungrateful, for the opportunity to study abroad had proved both an interesting and a fascinating experience.

No one could accuse her stepmother of neglecting familial duty or of failing to extend it to every sphere, Kris mused as she reflected on her recent stay at one of Paris's finest establishments, where skilled staff attempted to turn daughters of the rich and famous into well-educated, highly sophisticated individuals.

Dear Angela—beautiful, doll-like, and deadly in her pursuit of power and money; born with the knowledge that one went hand in hand with the other, and prepared to use every feminine wile to acquire it. Sven Laurensen hadn't stood a change. A widower at forty with a seven-year-old daughter, joint head of the multi-million-dollar Chayse-Laurensen industrial empire, he had been flattered, bemused, then bewitched, and within twelve months Angela had achieved her objective.

Three years later a massive coronary felled him in one terrible blow, leaving Angela with a large annuity, use of the Darling Point harbour-front home, a king's ransom in jewellery—and Kris.

Legally documented stipulations regarding Kris's care and education had been concisely detailed, and Angela exercised extreme care so as not to default on any one of them. Guardianship was shared jointly with Sven's business partner, and years at one of Australia's most prestigious private boarding schools had been followed by two years in Europe, one in Switzerland and the latter in France, to perfect, as Angela had so succinctly intimated, essential grooming, a comprehensive knowledge and appreciation of fashion, and a full mastery of all the essential social graces.

A year's absence had wrought few visible changes, Kris accorded as the Rolls entered the wide sweeping driveway. The gardens looked immaculate. Begonias provided a colourful display in their geometrically designed beds, the small satiny flowers ranging from white to palest pink, crimson to deep brilliant red. Shrubs vied for supremacy, each clipped and pruned to within a millimetre of its neighbour, and the lawns appeared velvet-smooth and green despite the summer heat.

Alighting from the car, she made her way towards the wide entrance foyer, and had barely reached the door when it was flung open and she was engulfed in an affectionate embrace.

'Kris, you're home!' Suzy Pemberton enthused with a suspicious dampness shimmering her eyes. 'I expect you're tired after such a long flight.'

Kris looked into those kindly features and felt close to tears herself. 'I am, a little. But nothing a shower and an early night won't fix. Where's Angela?'

'Why, *here*, darling.'

It didn't seem possible, but her stepmother looked even younger than her thirty-eight years, her dark lustrous hair caught in a careless knot atop her head, her fine-textured skin exquisitely made up, and, as always, her figure was nothing less than superb beneath a sheath of dark blue silk.

Angela Laurensen offered a hand in welcome, then presented a cool cheek for an obligatory greeting.

The pink pantsuit Kris had chosen to wear for the long international flight still looked crisp and clean, and her make-up had been removed and carefully re-applied an hour before touchdown. There was nothing whatsoever wrong with her appearance, yet despite years of instilled poise she knew herself to be no match for her beautiful stepmother.

'Come inside,' Angela bade with a slight smile, almost as if she was aware of the younger girl's pattern of thought. 'Sam will take care of your luggage, and I've already instructed Suzy to set up refreshments in the conservatory.' She lifted a languid hand to smooth back an imaginary hair, then it it fall to her side. 'You're very pale.'

'I didn't get much sleep on the plane,' Kris offered quietly, aware that she would never quite measure up to Angela's perpetual state of personified elegance. Despite an easy tolerance, there had always been a lack of closeness between them. Over the years she'd tried to bridge the gap and inevitably failed, becoming aware with growing maturity that her stepmother was self-orientated to a point where there was no room for another female in her life.

A faint frown was immediately replaced by an understanding smile. 'Those long flights are absolute hell. You'll want to shower and change. Shall we say half an hour?'

'Fine.' She did her best to inject an element of enthusiasm into her voice, then she crossed the marble-tiled floor and made her way downstairs.

Built against a sloping rockface, the house comprised no fewer than four levels, with skilful landscaping creating a further three levels leading down to the water's edge. The total effect portrayed monied elegance combined with imaginative flair, and its design had been featured in a variety of glossy magazines over the years depicting homes of Australia's rich and famous.

On reaching her suite Kris stepped inside and paused momentarily, glancing at the visual perfection evident in the pleasing blend of cool green and pale creamy-peach, co-ordinating drapes, soft-cushioned sofas, even the prints decorating the walls. The colour theme was carried through to the bedroom, with the *en suite* bathroom tiled floor to ceiling in muted shades of peach and cream. There was an oval spa-bath as well as the usual fitments, and without hesitation

Kris slid off her shoes, then slowly discarded her clothes.

Twenty minutes later she emerged from the spa feeling refreshed and relaxed. Wrapping a fluffy towel sarong-wise round her slim form, she completed her toilette, then moved into the bedroom.

Donning elegant silk underwear, she selected white cotton trousers and added a watermelon-pink top. Make-up was kept to a minimum, just moisturiser and a touch of gloss over her generously curved lips. Several tugs of the brush restored her hair to order, and she stood back to regard her mirrored reflection with analytical resignation.

Of average height and fashionably slender, she lacked true classical beauty. Fine bone structure gave her face a delicate air, enhanced by the bell-like frame of flaxen hair which was an inheritance from her Nordic ancestors. As were a pair of haunting vivid blue eyes, wide-spaced and fringed by thick dark lashes.

It all added up to an attractive image, but even the ugliest ducking could be made to appear a gracious swan when unlimited wealth supplied the finest in clothes and cosmetics. She was not unaware that she represented the product of an élite society; fashionably bred, educated, groomed, *finished*—if such a term was still applicable in today's era.

The precise purpose behind it all was something which caused vague feelings of unease, almost disquiet on occasion, for it seemed as if she had been deliberately channelled towards non-employment, proficient in several arts, but qualified in few.

Damn, Kris cursed silently. She'd been home

less than an hour, and already she was feeling vulnerable, on edge with a nervous tension that only Angela was able to evoke—inexplicable, but there nonetheless.

The conservatory was situated on the lowest level overlooking the pool, and Kris slid open one of the wide glass doors and wandered out on to the terrace, circumventing the tiled pool to pause at its balustraded edge.

A slight breeze teased the length of her hair, lifting it, and she tilted her head slightly so that the wayward strands fell back into place. The feel of the setting sun's warmth on her face acted like a soothing balm, and she drew in a deep breath, exulting in the slight tangy smell of the sea.

Slowly she let her gaze wander across the harbour towards the city, soft and hazy at this hour, the tall buildings standing like smoky-grey sentinels against a pink-streaked sky that slowly changed in hue to palest blue, then gold. Within minutes the gold would brighten to orange, a brilliant flaring before the sun dropped down beyond the horizon.

It was a sight she would never tire of viewing; her favourite city at sunset with its varied architecture, panoramic coves and peninsulas. Splashes of neon, multi-coloured flashing advertisements, vied for attention, their many signs forming a giant electronic patchwork, alive and beckoning. Mysterious, elusive, exciting, not unlike any other large city in the world, yet it held a magical quality, a familiarity that was inexplicably *home*.

'Ah, there you are.'

Kris turned at the sound of Angela's light voice, and a winsome smile hovered at the edge of her lips as she made her way indoors.

'I was admiring the view,' she explained simply,

taking the seat her stepmother indicated, sinking into its cushioned softness, aware of an inner weariness that stemmed from her body clock being at variance with a different time sequence.

A jug of iced fruit juice reposed on a nearby table, together with an assortment of wafer-thin crispbreads, mini-salads, and a delectable compote of fresh fruit.

'I thought something light would suffice,' Angela declared smoothly. 'You'll want to retire early.'

Why did the simplest discourse assume a thrust-and-parry quality, bringing forth a defensiveness that made her want to assert her own independence—even be contrarily the reverse of whatever Angela suggested?

'Would you mind if I just had a drink?' Kris demurred, tempering it with an apologetic smile. 'I'm not in the least hungry.'

Angela didn't bat so much as an eyelid. If anything, her perfectly painted lips curved into a conciliatory smile as she cajoled gently, 'Have something, darling.' Leaning forward, her movements gracefully smooth, she began dispensing portions into two heavy crystal dishes. 'Some fruit. Suzy made it especially for you— grapes, mango, melon, paw-paw, pineapple. It will refresh your palate.'

Kris felt too enervated to do anything but comply, and she accepted the small serving Angela offered, spooning the delectable segments into her mouth with docile obedience.

'I've arranged a party for Friday evening,' Angela began without preamble as she poured juice into two glasses. 'Just a few friends to welcome you home.'

Yours or mine? Kris felt inclined to query,

aware that her stepmother's idea of 'a few friends' inevitably meant at least thirty. It seemed safe to assume the guest list would read like a veritable *Who's Who* of Sydney's social echelon. Most of her friends were scattered throughout Australia, victims of a boarding-school existence, and were unlikely to attend. During the past two years she had lost touch with several, maintained an irregular correspondence at best with a few, and the one friend she considered anywhere near *close* had married a year ago and resided in Perth.

It would be equally hopeless to suppose informality would be observed—a barbecue with slightly over-cooked sausages, grilled steaks and an assortment of salads was far more to her liking than the sumptuous spread Angela would undoubtedly stage. Caviar, pâté, canapés and a positive gamut of hors d'oeuvres to tempt the most demanding palate would be presented, followed by a selection of delicacies that would take Suzy hours, if not the entire day, to prepare. French champagne would flow like water, and everyone would indulge in utterly meaningless chatter . . .

'You could try to appear enthusiastic, darling.'

Angela's smile was bright, but there was a degree of calculation in those dark eyes that made Kris feel distinctly wary.

'Thank you,' she murmured in polite response, sipping the cool, refreshing pineapple juice.

'I thought we might go shopping tomorrow. Not that you don't possess a number of suitable clothes,' her stepmother declared. 'But I have something—different in mind.' Her gaze narrowed slightly. 'You did visit some of the fashion houses while you were in Paris?'

Kris pictured her purchases—the shoes, accessories, the skirts and tops. Casual and off-the-peg, and not one of them possessing a famous designer label.

'I bought a few things,' she conceded, not wanting to elaborate and have a post-mortem held on the merits of her acquisitions.

Angela flicked her a swift, faintly sceptical glance, almost as if she knew there was nothing extravagantly expensive or worthy of particular note within her stepdaughter's luggage.

Or perhaps she was astute enough to realise that, while Kris had never indulged in flouting her by word or deed, assuming an apparent lack of interest in *haute couture* was one way of exerting independence.

Maybe it was simply because she wasn't cut out to be a bird of paradise, Kris concluded, aspiring instead to neat attire that was both comfortable and visually presentable. There was always the third alternative—that Angela spent more than enough on herself for both of them, and then some!

Not that there was any shortage of money, heaven forbid! Chayse-Laurensen chalked up *millions* in net profits every year. Only once had the graph faltered in its ever-upward surge towards increasing prosperity—five years previously, when Fletcher Chayse died in a fatal car accident, leaving his only son and heir to step into his awesome shoes. Now that faint hiccup was but a mere memory, accorded little more than a reassessment in top directorial management as Jared proved he was indeed his father's successor and more than worthy of assuming such a role. If anything, he had achieved the unachievable—that of steering Chayse-Laurensen on a straight course towards even greater success when other firms foundered and lost steam in troubled economic waters.

Kris had had immense respect for Fletcher Chayse, regarding him as a benevolent uncle. However, there was nothing remotely avuncular about his son, and it irked unbearably that Jared shared equal legal rights with Angela over her welfare.

Kris sipped the ice-cool tangy juice and reflected idly that at thirty-four Jared Chayse appeared to have it all. Hard, handsome and hateful, with a reputation that seemed to compound everything ever written about him. The press delighted in monitoring his every move, doubtless embellishing countless items of gossip, never failing to portray him as a ruthless rake who wielded power and broke hearts on a daily basis with shameless disregard.

'I've alerted Marguerite,' Angela's voice intruded, breaking into Kris's reverie. 'She has several selections which she assures me are eminently suitable.'

Kris managed not to wince visibly as she visualised the exclusive interior of Chez Marguerite in fashionable Double Bay. At the price Angela paid and the patronage she bestowed, Marguerite probably salaamed eternal gratitude every time Angela walked through her door.

'If you've finished, darling, I think you'd better get some sleep. You look positively worn out!'

That was nothing less than the truth, and Kris didn't attempt to argue as she replaced her glass and rose to her feet.

'We'll have a leisurely lunch,' Angela decided, 'then see what Marguerite has to offer.'

Beginning halfway through the day was an unheard-of concession, Kris mused idly, for Angela was an inveterate shopaholic whose interest extended far beyond clothes. Jewellery and paintings held top priority, but the list was seemingly endless, extending to antiques and *objets d'art*, adding to an impressive collection which, while being exceedingly expensive to maintain, was nonetheless gathered with astute selectivity, and there could be no doubt that most items had appreciated markedly in value over the years. An interest in bloodstock as well as the stockmarket, coupled with an active social life, ensured that her stepmother led an extremely busy existence.

'If you haven't surfaced by eleven, I'll have Suzy wake you.'

Kris knew it to be a dismissal, and with a singularly sweet smile she bade the older woman good night.

CHAPTER TWO

EVERYTHING bore the appearance of refined affluence. Floral arrangements, highlighted by majestic stands of gladioli surrounded by delicate ferns, long-stemmed carnations, roses, their colours carefully selected to blend with the décor, abounded throughout the huge formal lounge, adding artistic grace at a cost, Kris decided with a slightly jaundiced eye as she casually scanned several displays within her peripheral vision, sufficient to feed an average family for months.

Background music filtered through an elaborate quadraphonic system, muted, yet there none the less, the tapes chosen to set a preconceived mood, inviting relaxed enjoyment and merging pleasantly with the constant buzz of conversation.

Hired staff circulated among the guests with professional ease, proffering trays of exotic, tastefully prepared morsels of food, together with fresh glasses of champagne.

Angela, looking incredibly soignée in a Lapidus original—*calm*, when only two hours before she had been almost on the point of hysterics due to some minuscule domestic disruption, managed to exude unruffled charm as she moved from one group to another exulting in her role as hostess.

The evening had been skilfully engineered with the expertise of a highly organised event on which an incalculable amount of planning had been expended to ensure its success.

A faintly hollow laugh died in her throat as Kris reflected that her stepmother refused to identify with failure in any form, and that to imagine otherwise almost verged towards a heinous crime.

The party had been under way for several hours, and in that time Kris had dutifully made the round of guests, recounted with polite, even light wit, events of the past year, aware from the avid interest which such revelations evoked that it was her future which aroused speculation. In fact, it seemed that everyone attempted a deliberate ploy to determine her plans, and a smiling, non-committal response was received with less than satisfaction.

'You're looking decidedly pensive.'

Kris felt her eyes widen slightly, and she summoned a smile that radiated seeming warmth as she turned to meet the dark, gleaming gaze of the man standing less than a foot distant. As usual he'd managed to catch her unawares, and it made her feel uncommonly resentful.

'Jared. So nice of you to come.'

Sardonic humour flared briefly as his lips twisted to form a faintly mocking smile, deepening the slashing grooves in each cheek. 'Very politely spoken!'

His tall frame bore evidence of muscular litheness beneath its sheath of expensive suiting, and he managed to project an enviable aura of power—a dramatic mesh of male charisma and self-assurance that several men coveted but few achieved to any great degree.

'How was Paris?' An eyebrow slanted in quizzical query, his direct gaze assessing and vaguely analytical, and she was unable to suppress the tingle of electricity in her veins or still the faint quickening of her pulse.

It was maddening, but he had the strangest effect on her senses, making her aware of an elusive alchemy, an elemental sensuality she found vaguely frightening.

'Ah, now there's a good question,' Kris responded with forced lightness, and he laughed, a soft husky sound that sent shivers scudding in countless different directions.

'One you've no doubt answered at least a dozen times this evening,' he replied cynically.

'Twenty,' she corrected with undue solemnity, and glimpsed his amusement.

'That bad?' His teeth gleamed white for an instant, then became hidden beneath the curving slant of his mouth. 'You can humour me with a variety of anecdotes over dinner tomorrow night.'

She blinked, her long lashes flicking wide without any semblance of guile. *'Saturday?'* She forced her gaze to remain steady. 'Surely it can wait until next week? I'd hate to have my eyes scratched out by your latest——' she paused, then added with deliberate emphasis, 'companion.'

'Lover,' Jared substituted, not a whit disturbed by the delicate tinge of pink that coloured her cheeks.

Even the thought of that long sinewy body engaged in sexual exploits of any kind brought forth an acute stab of pain so intense that it seemed a tangible wound.

'I'm sure that should be plural,' Kris managed with remarkable calm, hating him.

His eyes narrowed faintly, and his expression became infinitely sardonic. 'Attempting to maintain more than one relationship at a time tends to present certain—complications, shall we say?'

'You would know,' she dismissed lightly, and lifting the fluted glass to her lips she sipped the excellent champagne, retaining a measure of *savoir-*

faire that lent credit to a number of highly paid tutors in a strict scholastic regime.

'Do you doubt it?'

His mocking drawl irked unbearably. 'I'm almost twenty-one,' she reminded him solemnly, meeting his level gaze with equanimity. Her chin lifted fractionally, and her eyes were steady, a brilliant sapphire blue, their depths reflecting perceptive clarity.

There was no visible change in his expression, except for the slight imperceptible lift of one eyebrow, then a crooked smile twitched the edges of his mouth. 'A self-professed woman of the world, hm?' he suggested with barely concealed cynicism.

'Hasn't attaining that state been the object both you and Angela have had in mind these past few years?' It was a double-edged barb meant to strike home, a veiled protest at having been despatched willy-nilly to two European capitals with scant regard for her own wishes. Somehow 'it's in your best interest' no longer carried much weight, and determination tinged with defiance lent her eyes a fiery sparkle, adding dimension to her attractive features.

'I've been away for almost a year, yet it seems like yesterday.' She cast the room a sweeping glance, and his eyes narrowed, their expression becoming slightly hooded.

'Another party, another occasion?'

Her smile widened in a bright facsimile. 'Angela excels in the role of hostess.'

'This evening was arranged solely for your benefit,' Jared reminded her drily.

'I'm most appreciative.'

'Yet unimpressed,' he drawled, and she gave a helpless shrug, stung by his chiding reproof.

'You make me sound like a spoilt little rich girl!'

His gaze was remarkably level, the dark grey depths presenting a veritable mask of inscrutability. 'Right on two counts.'

'Oh? With what exception?'

'In spite of a lifetime of apparent indulgence, I couldn't accord you spoilt,' he told her with soft detachment, and she sank mere inches in a mock curtsy.

'Good heavens—a compliment? I'm honoured.'

'So you should be,' Jared drawled with a certain wryness. 'It would have been all too easy for you to become a first-class brat.'

'Maybe you shouldn't speak too soon,' Kris declared fearlessly. 'I've just emerged from a metaphorical chrysalis, ready to spread my wings and fly. Sudden freedom can have a profound effect.'

Both brows rose in quizzical humour. 'A silken prison, hm?' His eyes gleamed with latent amusement. 'Somehow I can't believe it's been too much of a hardship.'

'Of course not. How could I possibly complain?' She lifted a hand in a negligent gesture, then let it fall to her side. 'Studying culture and couture in Paris, skimming down the slopes at Gstaad. But then you already know, don't you?'

'The surface details.'

'Ah.' If she didn't resort to mockery she'd probably hit him. 'Little things like how many times I required medical attention, visits to the dentist, sanctioning my allowance, credit card purchases.'

For a moment his expression became un-fathomable, then he queried gently, 'How is your arm?'

Do you really care? she felt like screaming. It

hurt like hell at the time, and in hospital no one came to visit me—at least, no one who really mattered. I never felt so alone in my life. Aloud, she said, 'I received your flowers. They arrived the same day as Angela's.' Dispensed by an identical florist, doubtless on instructions from his very capable secretary.

'I was in the States,' he informed her quietly, and for a moment she thought he sounded genuinely regretful. 'New York, Los Angeles, San Francisco. The news didn't reach me until a week after your accident.'

'By which time a report on my progress would have arrived, assuring you there was no cause for concern.' She hadn't intended to sound bitter, but the inference was there, and she felt immeasurably angry—with herself, for allowing him to catch a glimpse of the aching loneliness that had been an integral part of her for years.

Her glass was empty, a fact she noticed with vague detachment, and she felt her eyes widen as it was taken and another, part-filled, placed between her nerveless fingers.

Like magic, a waitress appeared out of nowhere, tray in hand, and Jared extracted a glass, proffering a smile that brought a dazzling response before the girl reluctantly moved away.'

'Drink it,' he bade indolently, and Kris obediently lifted the glass, hating the faint tremor that ran through her body as her lips touched the rim. There was something incredibly intimate about drinking from the same glass, knowing his mouth had savoured its contents only minutes before.

It was crazy, but she was totally unaware of the noise of milling chattering guests, music. It was as if she and Jared were alone, encapsulated for a few seconds in time where nothing else could intrude.

'Kris dear!' a breathy feminine voice penetrated a mere instant before a heavy, almost cloying perfume permeated the air. 'You can't monopolise this devastating man for too long. It simply won't do!'

She turned slowly, summoning a smile that contained polite reserve as she extended a gracious meeting.

Pamela Sloane, tall, svelte, a raven-haired beauty, daughter of *the* industrialist Sloane, successful model, and a positive man-eater. She and Jared were well matched—in looks and level of sophistication, and undoubtedly attuned to a sexual wavelength Kris could never hope to attain.

Innate good manners rose to the surface with scarcely any effort at all. 'Hello, Pamela. I trust you're enjoying yourself?' Turning her head slightly, she let her gaze encompass Jared. 'If you'll excuse me? I really must circulate.' Without waiting, she moved away and was almost immediately swallowed up by mingling guests.

Minutes later she replaced her empty glass, and shook her head in silent negation at the invitation to take another. Champagne tended to be deceptive, its golden bubbles seemingly innocuous as they slid effortlessly down her throat to explode with delayed impact some minutes later. Besides, she didn't need its false lift, nor feel particularly inclined to deal with the aftermath the following morning.

On reflection, it was an immensely successful evening, ending when the last remaining quartet of guests floated towards the front door amid a chorus of 'wonderful party, darling', 'thanks, sweetie', 'we'll arrange something *soon*', 'be in touch'.

As soon as the front door closed behind them,

Angela seemed visibly to relax, the effervescent, almost brittle mask dispensed with as Kris cast a quick glance at the exquisite ormolu clock on its nearby stand. Two-thirty. An hour prejudged to be neither too early nor too late, with the first departing guest not leaving until after one.

'Everyone enjoyed themselves,' she said quietly, and caught the swift gleam of satisfaction apparent as Angela inclined her head in silent agreement.

'You spoke to Jared.' It was a statement, and Kris wondered if anything escaped her stepmother's attention.

'For about ten minutes.' She strove to keep her voice casual, even uninterested.

'You're having dinner with him tomorrow night,' Angela declared, and at once resentment rose to the fore.

What was this—a conspiracy? 'I don't remember agreeing to go.'

One eyebrow arched in delicate appraisal. 'Jared distinctly said that he would collect you at seven.'

'Indeed?' How dared he expect her to comply meekly as if time spent in his company was a not-to-be-missed treat—worse, to go over her head and inform Angela, possibly before he'd extended the invitation! 'I may have made other plans.'

'Don't be tiresome, Kris.'

There was no denying the reproach evident, and she could easily have stamped her foot in retaliatory rage. She was no longer a *child*, dammit! 'Jared's obligation as guardian doesn't have to include courtesy dinners,' she retorted with a hint of defiance.

'There can be no question that you won't go,' Angela dismissed, and her gaze became faintly speculative as a slight frown momentarily furrowed her brow. 'The Zampatti white textured silk-dechine will do very well teamed with white accessories.'

It was on the tip of Kris's tongue to refuse openly, and she almost did, except that the sane, logical part of her brain urged capitulation. Dinner *à deux* with Jared was an innovation, and he was quite capable of pinning her down, if not tomorrow, then next week, or the week after that. It would be infinitely wiser to comply on this occasion and thereafter be restricted to seeing him briefly as a fellow guest at any one of several upcoming functions. Besides, Jared and Angela combined on one front presented a formidable force!

'In that case, I'll give in gracefully, thereby absolving him from further duty.' She hadn't meant to sound quite so cynical. Maybe it was the instinct of self-preservation, an inner fear that to have Jared stray from his familiar guardianship role would plunge her into a situation she might not be able to handle.

'Really, Kris, I'm surprised! Jared has a right to display an interest in your welfare. To consider refusing his invitation is impolite, to say the least.'

Lord, why argue? It only created tension, and besides, she was too tired to bother. Perhaps it was delayed jet-lag, or the result of attempting to do battle with two very strong-minded people, each equally intent that she should jump to their every command. Whatever the reason, she felt ill-equipped to deal with any further discourse tonight.

Aloud, she offered, 'I've agreed to go, so let's leave it at that, shall we?' She lifted a hand to her hair, absently smoothing back a stray tendril, and her eyes took on a smoky tinge as they became reflective and oddly resigned. 'Good night.'

* * *

Kris flicked an idle glance at her watch, then gave an audible sigh. Four o'clock. If she was to reach home, shower and be ready when Jared arrived, she would have to make a move.

The sun was extremely warm, its rays having a soporific effect on her supine, bikini-clad form, and she could easily have dozed for another hour.

In an act of unprecedented laziness she had risen from her bed just prior to midday, eaten a slice of wholemeal toast accompanied by freshly squeezed orange juice and followed by strong black coffee, then left a message with Suzy for Angela that she'd be at the beach for what remained of the afternoon. Without further delay she had selected keys for the Mercedes and headed for the North Shore, driving until she reached Sandy Bay.

Now her solitude must be abandoned, and with a groan she rose to her feet, donned a thin muslin top, slid sunglasses down on to her nose, then collected her towel and made her way to the car.

Once home, she paused only long enough to inform Suzy that she was back, then headed for the pool to cleave several vigorous lengths of its cool, clear depths before agilely levering her body on to the pool's edge.

With something akin to satisfaction she regarded the slim length of her legs, noting the lightly tanned skin, tinging pale gold and verging towards a deeper blush round her midriff where the sun hadn't touched for a number of months. A faint grimace twisted the edge of her mouth. Her skin was so pale that it must be obvious she'd come straight from a northern hemispheric winter. Still, a few weeks of careful sunbathing would soon provide an enviable tan.

Water slid down her back, easing to droplets of

moisture as her hair dried beneath the late afternoon sun, and she let her head fall back as she smoothed her fingers through its shaped length. Then she stood easily to her feet, wrapped the towel round her slim curves and retraced her steps indoors.

The cool needle-spray of the shower revitalised her pores, and she shampooed her hair, then applied conditioner to restore its natural silkiness, taking much longer than necessary before shutting off the water and emerging from the luxuriously appointed cubicle.

Her toilette completed, she slipped into fresh underwear, then donned a silken wrap and set about styling her hair with the blowdrier. Nails were given two coats of iridescent pearl lacquer before they met with her critical satisfaction. Make-up came next, and she applied moisturiser, then a peach-tinted base, before skilfully outlining her eyes with varying shades of blue. Highlighters added depth, and several applications of mascara lent her lashes a dark lustrous length.

It was almost six-thirty when she slid back the mirrored doors of her wardrobe, and her fingers hovered over several suitable dresses before settling on Angela's preferred Zampatti original.

Pencil-slim heeled shoes in softest white kid, together with a matching evening purse, were her only accessories, and she fastened a diamond pendant on a fine gold chain round her neck, added matching studs to each earlobe, then examined her overall appearance in the long chevalled mirror.

Her reflected image stared back, silent and slightly pensive, a visual attestation of perfection. Animation was the only missing ingredient, and she watched with detached interest as her mouth curved to form a musing smile. Was it imagination, or could she actually *hear* Mademoiselle Jacqueline's voice impart an oft-repeated injunction? '*Eyes*. Remember always the eyes. Practise the mood you wish to project.'

Unbidden, the blue depths acquired a vivacious sparkle, a clarity that portrayed intense interest, until the image became alive.

The last remaining touch was perfume, and she chose the elusive magic of Jean-Louis Scherrer, anointing several pulse-beats before making her way from the room amid a delicate cloud of wafting fragrance.

Jared had already arrived, and he turned as she entered the lounge, watching her progress beneath a mask of studied indolence.

He looked totally at ease, a part-filled tumbler of whisky held in one hand. Superb tailoring accented his muscular frame and gave emphasis to an enviable breadth of shoulder, while snowy linen drew attention to deeply-tanned skin and dark, almost black, well-groomed hair.

Angela stood close by, radiating vivacious charm, and looking incredibly soignée in an Oldfield designer outfit that emphasised her startling beauty.

'Ah, there you are, darling,' purred Angela, her eyes taking in Kris's appearance, analysing and according silent approval at a glance.

Feeling as if she was an interesting specimen on display, Kris offered Jared a polite greeting, then moved towards a nearby armchair and sank gracefully into its comfortable depths.

'Charming.' His eyes tinged with musing warmth, and a sloping smile tugged the corners of his mouth. 'What can I get you to drink?'

He might have been describing a child dressed in

party finery, and it irked to be relegated to the ranks of juvenility.

Acquired poise enabled her to utter a polite acknowledgment, and her eyes were extraordinarily steady as she held his gaze. 'Something long and cool—white vermouth with lemonade.' One felt the need to be decisive in Jared's company, and project an infinite degree of assurance. Anything less inevitably resulted in a shocking lack of self-confidence.

Kris didn't know whether to be relieved or apprehensive when Jared indicated some ten minutes later that they should leave, and it wasn't until they were in the car that she sought to determine their destination.

'Anxious for the evening to be over and done with, before it has even begun?'

His voice was dry and vaguely cynical, and she found herself responding carefully. 'Curious.'

'About where I'm taking you?'

He was being deliberately facetious, and she glanced towards him, noting the inherent vitality evident, coupled with a trace of ruthlessness beneath the sophisticated veneer.

'I'm sure your choice of restaurant is impeccable.'

He shot her a glance that held a degree of lazy tolerance. 'I'm relieved to learn you trust my judgment.'

'Your expertise has to be without question,' she returned sweetly, and incurred a deep probing glance as the car paused at an inner city intersection.

An imperceptible shiver slithered down the length of her spine, and Kris lifted a hand to her hair, smoothing back a stray tendril in a strangely defensive gesture.

'I assume you have no intention of qualifying that remark,' he remarked drily, and she watched with detached fascination as he manoeuvred the sleek Aston Martin through the stream of evening traffic. His hands were broad with long tapered fingers, infinitely masculine yet possessing a tactile sensuality she found disturbing.

To feel so inordinately vulnerable was crazy, and she projected light amusement into her tone, parrying almost wryly, 'Must I?'

In the dim evening dusk his expression was difficult to determine, but she detected cynical amusement as he drawled, 'I'll allow you to get away with it—this time.'

'How magnanimous of you!'

The car gained entrance to an underground carpark and slid easily into an empty space. With graceful fluidity Kris unbuckled her seatbealt, then slipped out and closed the door behind her, turning to send him a stunning smile across the highly polished metal roof.

Jared locked the car and crossed to her side, catching hold of her elbow in a light clasp, and she was all too aware of the sudden quickening of her pulse in recognition of his proximity.

'I'm not particularly hungry.' It was nothing less than the truth, and she evaded his penetrating glance, beginning to wish she'd never agreed to dine with him in the first place.

'A glass of wine will sharpen your appetite,' he declared, summoning the elevator.

The slowly revolving restaurant atop the city's highest tower revealed breathtaking views from every window, and the pinpricks of streetlights below formed a delicate tracery interspersed with bright flashing neon. Soon the sky would darken into inky blackness, and the vividness of multi-coloured lights would intensify, providing a beautiful backdrop to complement the restaurant's delightful décor.

With suitable deference the *maître d'* ushered them to their table, saw them seated, then summoned the wine steward, and it wasn't until Kris had sipped an excellent vintage Chardonnay that Jared deferred to her choice from an extensive menu.

'Seafood,' she deliberated thoughtfully, scanning the impressive list. 'Prawns in garlic sauce, followed by a grilled sole with a garden salad.' She closed the leather-bound menu and handed it to the waiter standing patiently while Jared deliberated over his preferred selection.

'Oysters Kilpatrick, followed by grilled barramundi with salad.' He cast Kris an enquiring glance. 'Herb or garlic bread?'

She indicated that the choice was his, then took a generous sip of wine as she let her gaze wander slowly round the room.

It was well patronised, and the piped music provided a relaxing background to the muted chatter of fellow diners.

'Tell me about your year.'

Kris replaced her glass carefully, then slowly met his level gaze. 'A brief résumé, Jared? For the sake of conversation?'

He looked totally at ease, the epitome of an urbane sophisticate. 'You doubt my interest is genuine?'

She endeavoured to keep her voice light. 'As what, specifically? Friend, guardian of my inheritance, or because you feel duty-bound to show concern?'

His gaze narrowed and assumed an inscrutability, a watchfulness that was somehow worse than any patronising amusement. 'Must there be a distinction?'

Answering that could be decidedly dangerous, she thought silently, feeling for a breathtaking second as if she'd suddenly lost her senses. It had to be the effect of vintage wine on an empty stomach!

Somehow she forced herself to hold his gaze as she effected a slight shrugging gesture. 'What shall we discuss? The weather? How many points Chayse-Laurensen has gained on the sharemarket? A review of any acquisitions? The latest fiscal report?'

One eybrow slanted sardonically, and she caught a slight gleam apparent in his eyes as he began a drawling dissertation.

'Chayse-Laurensen experienced a successful year, with the projected percentage of net profit exceeding its original provisional estimation. A slight upsurge in the economy has shown renewed buoyancy in the building industry, marginally increasing previous values, so that properties acquired by our subsidiaries when the market was at its lowest ebb are now beginning to prove their investment potential. The Gold Coast is one area which is gaining particular interest with the completion of Hilton's Jupiter's Casino, three multi-level hotel complexes under construction and several other projects having been given approval. Asian investment in several sectors is an interesting factor, and tourism is gaining both renewed attention and some acclaim due to specific and astute advertising.' Lines radiated from the corners of his eyes as he shot her a quizzical smile. 'Shall I continue with some other meaningless financial information, or shall we call a mutual halt?'

'That effectively takes care of round one.' A soft bubbly laugh rose to the surface, and her eyes sparked with blue intensity. 'What's next?'

'You were going to tell me about Paris.'

He was nothing if not persistent, and a flippant response rose to her lips, then died as she caught sight of his intent regard. 'You're no stranger to France's capital city, Jared,' she managed quietly. 'If you want to know if I enjoyed myself while at Mademoiselle Jacqueline's establishment, the answer has to be yes. It enabled me to polish up and perfect my French and to become proficient in the fine arts, including cuisine. It was a very productive course, and undoubtedly worth every cent.'

'That wasn't what I meant.'

'What do you want me to say? That I hated every minute, had no appreciation of some of the world's most celebrated works of art, and failed to perceive the elusive magic that is Paris itself?'

He chose to ignore the faint edge of resentment in her voice, and she met his gaze with equanimity, a tiny devil tempting her to resort to provocation.

'Are you afraid I may have fallen desperately in love with some totally unsuitable young man?'

'The very reason for selecting Mademoiselle Jacqueline was her awareness of the necessity for security with regard to her pupils,' Jared said drily, and Kris's eyes narrowed faintly.

'I see,' she said tightly. 'Every movement monitored—with the utmost discretion, of course.'

He took his time answering, and she felt close to screaming with vexed indignation at his and Angela's machinations.

'You are a prime target for fortune-hunters,' he revealed slowly.

'Oh, really!' she expostulated. 'Are you seriously

expecting me to believe I could have been the victim of a kidnap attempt?'

'Such methods are for the extremists, and usually politically activated. No, that was a remote possibility, especially when there were other pupils far more susceptible.'

'Next, you'll tell me I shared lodgings with royalty.'

'Try the daughter of one of the Arab States' wealthiest Sheiks, an English countess and an Austrian princess,' Jared mocked. 'Not to mention several young ladies whose fathers head vast consortiums throughout America and Europe.'

Kris swallowed quickly, mentally recalling each member of their select group, endeavouring to perceive who might have fallen into any one of those categories.

'Strict measures were taken to ensure that each of the girls in question used a family surname so that their identities remained unknown to all but a trusted few,' he continued, watching each fleeting expression on her expressive features.

'We were escorted to various functions, so I presume our partners had already been screened?' She felt an uncontrollable urge to lash out and hit him, and her knuckles clenched white beneath the napkin on her lap. In fact, she could barely trust herself to speak without resorting to anger. 'Young men specifically informed that their attentions were to be maintained at a platonic level. That's despicable!' she snapped angrily.

'A necessary precaution,' Jared corrected, and as if the matter was of no further concern he calmly finished his starter and bade her do likewise, so that the waiter could serve their main course.

Her appetite gone, she scarcely did justice to the

prawns, and merely picked at the fish and the crisp salad when it came. Succulent strawberries, tangy pineapple and delectable segments of melon were forked absently into her mouth and swallowed with little enthusiasm, while Jared took a selection from the proffered cheeseboard, and she declined both the liqueur and coffee, hating his unhurried ease.

Perhaps she should have expected the explosion of flashbulbs, for there were any number of photographers who made their living by frequenting numerous restaurants in the hope of discovering something suitably newsworthy to sell to various publications. From the young man's beaming deference, finding Jared Chayse was nothing less than a major coup. Without doubt it would make at least one of the city's newspapers within a matter of days, emblazoned with a suitable caption. It had happened before, occasions when she had been described as his attractive ward, the late Sven Laurensen's daughter, Angela Laurensen's stepdaughter—rarely as *Kris* Laurensen.

'Would you prefer to stay here, or go on to a nightclub?' asked Jared.

'I'd like to go home,' she declared without preamble, and saw one eyebrow slant in studied appraisal.

'It's barely ten,' Jared drawled, and she was driven to retort swiftly, 'You invited me to dinner. Why prolong the evening?'

'I thought we might call in at a nightclub for an hour or two.'

The prospect of another few hours in his company didn't appeal. Jared Chayse in small doses she could deal with, but there was a stalking quality apparent in his manner which was distinctly unnerving. For some unknown reason she had the instinctive sensation that he was playing a game, biding time for the right moment to pounce.

'I'd prefer not, if you don't mind.'

Reaching for the proffered bill, he signed it, pocketed the duplicate, then queried silkily, 'Shall we go?'

There was little Kris could do but comply, and she preceded him to the elevator, aware of his presence in the confines of the electronic cubicle all the way down to the car park.

Within minutes the Aston Martin was purring smoothly along the city streets, and she sank back against the opulent leather seat, letting her head rest comfortably as she idly scanned the passing shops. The pavements held a number of strolling people, some like themselves who had dined nearby, others having just vacated one of several cinemas and intent on finding somewhere to eat.

The car cruised steadily east, and it wasn't until they passed Darling Point that Kris turned towards him with a startled query framing her lips.

'Where are you taking me?'

'Double Bay.'

Realisation dawned, and her eyes became stormy with resentment. 'Must you be so overbearing?'

He spared her a swift glance, and in the reflected streetlight his expression was infinitely cynical. 'It's rarely necessary,' he said dryly, and she hid a faint grimace.

No, it wouldn't be. His—*women* vied for his attention with an avidness that was sickening, then displayed eager anticipation of any favours he chose to bestow, their willingness to please only too blatantly obvious.

Minutes later the car slid to the kerb in the main Double Bay thoroughfare, and for a moment Kris considered remaining motionless, then common sense prevailed.

Jared turned his head slightly, then leant his arm against the steering wheel as he watched the flicker of emotions chase across her expressive features. 'This particular nightclub opened a few months ago, and from all reports is very good,' he drawled.

She turned towards him and met his cool enigmatic gaze. 'Next you'll tell me you simply want to check the place out for yourself.'

A faint smile lurked in the depths of his dark eyes and his mouth curved with wry humour. 'Indulge me.'

'You could always deliver me home, then come back on your own,' Kris declared evenly in a last-ditch effort to flout him.

Fleeting irritation showed momentarily, then he proffered smoothly, 'I don't frequent nightclubs in search of feminine company.'

'Why should you?' she parried sweetly. 'When you have a legion of women filling every page of your little black book.'

'Are we going to sit here and pander words all night?' There was a hint of steel apparent, and with a slight shrug she unbuckled her seatbelt, then slipped from the car to standing waiting on the pavement as he locked up.

The nightclub was filled to capacity, making its intimate confines seem even more crowded, and finding a seat became impossible, so after a few minutes of fruitless searching they ordered drinks from the bar and then stood sipping them. Conversation was precluded by the proximity of the resident band, and Jared shot Kris a wry glance which she returned with faint amusement.

'On a popularity rating, it has to score a maximum ten.'

He replaced his glass and quizzed somewhat dryly, 'Shall we try the dance floor?'

It was a clear choice of being crushed at the bar or jostled on the floor, and Kris determined in favour of the latter. Although afterwards she wasn't sure it was such a good idea, for the sheer volume of patrons gracing the small space meant a much closer contact with Jared than she would have preferred.

She had danced with him before, felt the firm clasp of his hand and the strength of his arms as they held her, but for some reason tonight there was a subtle difference evident. A heightened awareness of the fine textured material beneath her fingers, the elusive tang of his exclusive cologne melding with the indisputable aura of power he managed to exude. It was the composite of a well-honed muscular frame at its peak of physical fitness, allowing natural grace of movement which had an almost hypnotic effect on her senses.

Beneath his touch she resisted the temptation to close her eyes and become lost in a complexity of emotions that were too difficult to define.

It was no wonder women fell for him, she acknowledged wryly. Jared Chayse was the embodiment of every superlative depicting male charisma, which, combined with unlimited wealth, made him one of Australia's most sought-after bachelors. The fact that he had not as yet taken any one of several eminently suitable women as his wife gave cause for conjecture, and the press had a field day if perchance the same woman graced his arm more than twice at any social function.

'You're very quiet.'

Kris glanced up and met his dark enigmatic gaze with equanimity. 'I didn't realise you wanted to indulge in polite conversation,' she answered, and felt his hold tighten fractionally.

'You're not in the least sorry,' drawled Jared, making his way steadily towards the edge of the dance floor.

She allowed him to lead her to the foyer, then walked at his side to the car. Surprisingly it was almost midnight, the late evening air warm with just the merest hint of a breeze fanning in from the sea. She could smell the salty tang, a sharp freshness that was lacking during the day.

Ten minutes later Jared brought the powerful car to a halt in the gravelled driveway, and Kris smothered a sigh of relief that the evening was at an end. Not that she hadn't enjoyed herself, for it had been extremely pleasant, and she said as much, then thanked him with just the correct degree of warm civility.

'Good night, Krista.'

There was a hint of veiled mockery evident, and her eyes widened measurably. Only her father had ever called her Krista. It was a beautiful name, given in memory of her paternal grandmother, and somehow hearing it fall from Jared's lips was sheer sacrilege. The desire to upbraid him was strong, and for a moment she almost did, then she decided not to give him the satisfaction.

Without a word she reached for the doorclasp, slid out from the car, closed the door behind her, then walked the few steps to the vividly lit front entrance, inserted her key, and deigned not to accord him so much as a backwards glance.

It wasn't until she had locked up and snapped off the lights that she heard the car start up, and she moved to the security panel, waiting until the appropriate instrument light stopped blinking before switching on the alarm system. Then she made her way down to her suite.

CHAPTER THREE

THE next few days were hectic as Kris allowed herself to be caught up in a whirl of pre-Christmas festivities which encompassed two luncheons, a charity fashion parade and late afternoon cocktails. And that excluded the evenings, for it was then that the city's élite society excelled itself. Angela's social calendar appeared formidable, and Kris could only admire her stepmother's verve and vivacity as she manipulated invitations into her busy schedule with enviable charm. It was an acquired talent, and one which Angela had perfected to the nth degree, earning her an undisputed reputation as one of Sydney's most respected hostesses.

Jared's presence at the Sorrensons' elegant Vaucluse mansion on Wednesday evening made it the third time Kris had seen him in as many days, and the fact that he arrived alone elicited speculative conjecture, for the absence of a beautiful blonde or brunette clinging to his side was a hitherto unknown occurrence.

A faint perplexed frown creased her brow as she sipped the innocuous concoction Simon Sorrenson had presented her with only moments before.

'Really, Kris, you haven't taken notice of a thing I've said,' that young man complained in an aggrieved tone, and she turned slightly, giving him her undivided attention.

'On the contrary,' she soothed with a witching smile. 'It must be terribly difficult having to bear with so many biased buffoons within your father's consortium when you have a multitude of innovative alternatives to implement.'

'Now you're making fun of me!'

Oh dear, for such an academically brilliant young man, he was quite obtuse when it came to human frailties. 'I think,' she ventured gently, softening her words so as not to hurt his feelings, 'you should bear in mind their collective experience and present your ideas accordingly.'

'But dammit, I'll be in charge one day. They have to realise that,' Simon burst out with more than a touch of arrogance, and Kris sighed, beginning to feel vaguely sympathetic towards Harvey Sorrenson's key personnel.

Her attention wandered, her eyes skimming the room as she unconsciously sought out a particular dark, well-groomed head, and her heart gave a dull lurch as she saw Jared seemingly engrossed in conversation with Angela.

Her glamorous stepmother looked positively radiant, her simply-styled black gown complementing a flawless figure, and self-assurance oozed from every pore of her youthful-looking skin.

By comparison Kris felt immature, despite the elegant ice-blue creation that graced her slender curves, and she could only envy the older woman's élan. With anyone else she had no difficulty in projecting a sophisticated image, but beneath Jared's shrewd and often inscrutable gaze she felt incredibly young.

At that moment he looked up, and the breath caught in her throat as a slow smile tugged the edge of his mouth. She watched in idle fascination as he murmured something to Angela, then gradually eased his way across the room.

A prickle of apprehension made itself felt in the pit of her stomach, and she launched into an

animated divertissement that caused poor Simon
to almost gape with surprise.

'Kris,' Jared greeted her with easy urbanity, and
turning towards her companion he gave a brief
nod in acknowledgment. 'Simon.'

'We must get together. Tomorrow night?
Perhaps you'd care to have dinner with me, then
go on to a nightclub somewhere?' Simon asked,
and Kris opened her mouth to refuse only to hear
Jared respond with considerable tolerance,

'Kris is dining with me. Another time, perhaps?'

She just barely managed to contain her surprise,
and her eyes sparked a brilliant blue at his high-
handedness. Not that she particularly wanted to
accept Simon's invitation, but to have Jared
intervene was an impossible liberty.

Simon cast them each a cool studied glance,
made his excuses and melted out of sight.

'You have no right——'

'My dear Kris, you would have been bored to
tears,' Jared drawled.

He was amused, damn him! 'That's no excuse,'
she said tightly. 'Besides, I've no intention of
dining with you!'

'I insist. Mrs Hadfield is looking forward to it,'
he informed her imperturbably. An eyebrow
slanted with deliberate mockery. 'You wouldn't
consider disappointing her, surely?'

His housekeeper was an angelic Scot who had
faithfully served the Chayse family for years, and
as Jared's ward Kris had long been regarded with
affection.

'You ride roughshod over everyone, don't you?'
Kris said fiercely as a concession to resigned
capitulation, and glimpsed his slow smile.

'Six o'clock. I'll collect you before leaving the city.'

Her blue eyes widened perceptibly. 'That won't

be necessary,' she declined angrily, feeling unaccountably outraged. 'Sam can drive me.' Damn his teasing arrogance, his total assurance in achieving his objective—whatever that happened to be!

Just once she'd like to see him at a loss for words—to feel as rawly vulnerable as he was able to make her feel. It was something she'd been aware of for years, she conceded with a certain wryness. A heightened sensitivity that had merely magnified as she had progressed through the awkward teenage stage, and had failed to lessen in intensity as she was permitted to date. Socialise, she corrected, remembering each and every occasion with remarkable clarity.

'Perhaps we should circulate,' she declared, and fleeting amusement appeared in his eyes.

'Afraid to be seen talking to me for too long, Kris?'

'Self-preservation,' she responded steadily. 'I've no desire to have my eyes scratched out by Pamela—or any one of your several *friends*,' she concluded with delicate emphasis, tempering it with a singularly sweet smile. 'If you'll excuse me?'

'I'll permit you to get away with it, this time,' Jared asserted mockingly, and she turned and determinedly made her way towards a group of people who immediately swallowed her up in their midst amid sparkling innocuous chatter.

Half-an-hour later she glimpsed Jared talking to a glamorous redhead, and saw them leave together within minutes. Presumably bound for his apartment in Double Bay, she decided darkly, hating the wayward trend of her thoughts and her own damnable imagination.

It was a relief when Angela intimated a desire to depart, and once home Kris bade her stepmother good night and retired to her room.

*   *   *

Jared's home was situated in Clontarf on the northern side of the harbour; a magnificent house reminiscent of an elegant European château, constructed in pale grey-and-white weathered brick and built with meticulous attention to detail. Standing high above the Spit, it commanded a panoramic view and boasted every amenity for luxurious living. Set on two blocks of land, it was enhanced by attractive landscaping and reached by a circular driveway.

Kris wondered idly who Jared had invited as her fellow guests as she preceded Gordon Hadfield through the vaulted entrance. A sweeping staircase led up to a mezzanine floor which contained a study, library and three guest suites. Four bedrooms each with a bathroom *en suite* occupied the uppermost floor, leaving the entire ground level for formal and informal entertaining. An abundance of Italian slab marble was evident in all the reception rooms, and rich Chinese rugs covered highly polished wood floors. There were several hand-cut crystal chandeliers and wall sconces, complementing what she considered to be the most gracious of all his three personal residences. At least, it was the one in which she felt most at home. The Double Bay penthouse suite was a showplace, which she knew to be primarily a bachelor pad, and a third contemporary-style country retreat nestled among bush-clad hills within sight of the Blue Mountains a few hours' drive west of the city, used infrequently whenever he wanted total relaxation.

'Jared won't be long. He was held up at the office, and arrived only a few minutes ago,' Gordon Hadfield explained as he led her into the spacious lounge. 'Can I get you a drink?'

Kris crossed the room and paused beside the

wide-glassed window to watch the numerous small craft anchored inside the middle harbour. 'Wine,' she said without hesitation 'A dry white.'

He filled a fluted glass and brought it to her.

'I'll take this through to the kitchen and drink it while I talk to Mrs Hadfield.'

She found her way to the housekeeper's domain with familiar ease, and greeted the small middle-aged woman with an affectionate hug, then she wrinkled her nose in silent appreciation of a number of tantalising aromas permeating the air.

'Hm, I daren't hazard a guess! Can I help?'

'If you must do something, you can finish setting the table, but first tell me about your French finishing school.'

'I'll give you a condensed version,' Kris teased, her eyes sparkling with mischief. 'Otherwise the guests will arrive and Jared will think I've deserted him.'

'Unlikely, as you're the only guest, but then you're almost family and not really a guest at all,' the older woman replied in accented brogue, and Kris barely contained her surprise, unsure whether to feel relieved or vaguely resentful that Jared intended they should dine alone.

A faint niggle of apprehension rose insidiously to the surface and refused to abate as she skimmed over her year in France, regaling Mrs Hadfield with several amusing anecdotes, before she crossed into the elegant dining-room to attend to the table.

Jared appeared just as she completed the task, looking rugged and invincible in impeccable light-grey trousers and a navy blue silk shirt.

Kris toyed with her drink, launching into animated small talk, and she felt immeasurably relieved when dinner was announced.

Although she did the excellent vichyssoise justice and ate the smoked salmon with its accompanying sauce, by the time Mrs Hadfield served the blanquette de veau her appetite had waned to the point of non-existence. Against her better judgment she accepted a small serving, but although it was exquisitely delicious she was only able to manage a mouthful or two.

'Not hungry?'

She looked up and caught Jared's slanted glance, offering a slight negative shake of her head and tempering it with a vague smile. 'I really can't eat another thing.'

His eyes narrowed, and he reached for the wine, only to pause as she quickly placed a hand over her glass. 'No?' A smile curved his generous mouth, and a gleam of amusement became apparent as he refilled his glass. 'My dear Kris, if I didn't know better I could almost imagine you to be nervous. Are you?'

This was a little too close to the truth for comfort, and she summoned a seemingly careless smile, directing at him a level look that doubtless didn't fool him in the slightest. He'd always possessed the ability to see beyond her projection of innate good manners, dissecting and dispensing her veneer of quiet poise with an ease that was galling. To allow anyone that power merely magnified her sense of acute vulnerability. At seventeen she had been able to bear it, but at almost twenty-one having a man of Jared's calibre see into her soul was nothing less than an embarrassment.

Such introspection was regressive and dangerous, and although she had no desire to meet him on equal terms it became imperative to pretend a modicum of panache. Hadn't that been

what the past two years were all about? The
amount expended in fees alone at each establishment was exorbitant enough to guarantee that their
pupils emerged as perfectly groomed, polished
young ladies skilled in the art of being adept in
any given situation.

'Wary,' Kris corrected lightly, holding his gaze.
'Somehow I can't help thinking all this is leading
up to something.'

'Now what gives you that idea?' he drawled, and
she leaned back in her chair in a graceful fluid
movement that gave the impression she was
completely at ease.

'Past experience,' she reminded him carefully.

He surveyed her for what seemed an age, until
she almost wilted beneath his intent appraisal.

'You believe I have some particular motive in
mind?' he queried at last, and she felt a *frisson* of
apprehension slip stealthily down her spine.

'Are you going to deny that you do?' Kris parried, watching as he lifted the crystal glass to
his mouth. His action held the precision of a
master chess player, portraying studied deliberation combined with a degree of calculation she
found distinctly chilling. It was crazy to feel she
was awaiting sentence, but in a way it was true,
with Jared and Angela presiding as judge and jury
over her fate for—how long this time? Another
year? Doing what? Surely not another finishing
school? That would only be duplicating everything
she had already been taught. The nerves in her
stomach tightened into a painful ball, playing
havoc with her digestive processes, and for a wild
moment she thought she might actually be sick.

'Relax,' Jared bade brusquely, his expression
shuttered beneath lowered lashes. 'I'm not your
executioner.'

She swallowed painfully, and her eyes held a strange haunting quality as she fought for control. 'No? Merely my guardian, trustee of my inheritance, and self-appointed mentor.'

'That bothers you?'

Bother was too mild a descriptive, and too singular! During the past seven years, when awareness of Jared Chayse had first risen damnably to the surface, his influence over her life, her emotions, covered such a complexity of impressions they were too numerous to evaluate. Attempting to define them had interrupted her studies and kept her awake at nights.

'I recognise the necessity,' she admitted stiffly, and his smile was entirely without humour as he drawled,

'I imagine I should be grateful for that, at least.'

Now he was being hatefully cynical, and Kris didn't find it difficult to adopt a cool facade. 'Are you intending to keep me in suspense while you progress through dessert and the cheeseboard, followed by your favourite liqueur?'

'Delay the agony? I think not. Watching you fidget for the next half-hour or so would destroy my appetite.'

'Am I supposed to guess?' Her eyes became brilliant with resentment. 'Surely I'm not to be Angela's companion on the social circuit, dogging her footsteps in an endless round of luncheons, cocktails and shopping?' As that brought no response, she struck off an imaginary list. 'No? Thank heaven for small mercies. Let me see,' she pondered with unaccustomed sarcasm. 'There must be several doors you can open. Even set me up in business. A boutique, perhaps? Or maybe I might be permitted to occupy an office within the portals of Chayse-Laurensen checking non-essential details while taking out an enormous salary?'

He shifted in his chair, his expression bleak and unyielding. 'You don't need the money, and to consider employment elsewhere would cause a ripple of amusement throughout the business world.'

'Since I'm not to be a social butterfly, run my own business or be gainfully employed, my mind is a hopeless blank over an alternative.'

Jared dispensed with his drink and waited while Mrs Hadfield removed his plate and served dessert, then when that good woman had left for the kitchen he looked at the visually perfect crème caramel before pushing it to one side and reached for the cheeseboard. Taking his time, he cut into the Camembert, selected a water biscuit and ate both with enjoyment.

'You've left out marriage,' he informed her in a voice devoid of emotion, and for a few heart-stopping seconds Kris just stared at him, her eyes wide, their depths assuming a haunting luminous quality as her brain assimilated the enormity of his words.

'*My God,*' she breathed at last. 'I suppose I should have guessed! The exclusive private education, finishing schools—all to achieve one goal.' She felt cold, despite the warmth of the summer evening. 'Like a prize bitch taught to behave correctly, then mated with a sire of equal breeding.' Her eyes filled with brilliant fire and the sheen of unshed tears. 'I assume you and Angela have already vetted a selection of highly successful *wealthy* young men to be presented for my approval?' Her chin tilted slightly, and unconsciously she squared her slim shoulders as she sat more upright on her chair. 'Am I permitted a vacation first, or is the marriage campaign to begin immediately?'

'There was never any question of whom you would marry, merely *when*,' Jared responded with deceptive softness.

Kris was shaking inside, hurt and mindlessly angry. The atmosphere between them became electric as he caught her gaze and held it, his eyes darkly inscrutable, watching, *waiting* with a diabolical patience as her expressive features slowly registered a gamut of fleeting emotions.

Not—*him*? In all her wildest nightmares she had never envisaged what he was hinting. Jared Chayse and Kris Laurensen. Together, their individual fortunes would cement a financial empire, thus preserving it for a further generation. The logistics of such a union were abundantly clear. Stocks on the share market would flutter and soar, reaching new heights, promoting even greater equity.

'The possibility must surely have occurred to you?' he drawled, and her pulse seemed to leap and throb into frantic life, whether in fear, excitement, or a mixture of both she was unsure.

'Would you believe—*no*?' Tension knotted unenviably in her stomach until it became a tangible pain, and she wondered how she could sound so calm when inside she was a mess, her nerves shredding to pieces with every passing second.

'At least each of us can be sure neither is pursuing the other for material gain,' Jared remarked drily.

'One must always be on guard against the number of fortune-hunters, male and female, who would do anything to get their hands on our millions.' She was being horribly sarcastic, but she no longer cared. 'So, rather than be culled by some greedy money-grubbing adventurer with an eye to indulging in a life-long spending spree, *we* ensure that our joint inheritance remains sacrosanct.' She paused, her breathing ragged. 'Presuming I should agree, what of *our* children, Jared?' she queried with unaccustomed bitterness. 'Surely you can't foresee being able to dictate *their* lives?'

His eyes narrowed, although his gaze was no less intent. 'I'm talking about now, not twenty-five or thirty years into the future.'

'And naturally I'm expected to see the wisdom of your proposal,' she essayed cynically.

'I imagine you're sensible enough to weigh up all the advantages.'

The thought of becoming Jared's wife, sharing his bed, needed careful consideration before making any definite commitment. Part of her wanted to refuse, *now*. Yet there was a wild reckless streak urging acceptance, daring her to be swept into an emotional vortex and be damned to the consequences.

'Forgive me,' she said at last, her voice filled with icy anger. 'I don't feel inclined to be sensible.'

Jared reached out and and selected the smallest of three exquisitely cut Waterford glasses within easy reach, filling it with a measure of Cointreau and swirling the rich-coloured liquid absently as he subjected her to a faintly brooding appraisal.

'There is an aspect you should be aware of—a legal technicality regarding Sven's will.' He appeared to choose his words with the utmost care. 'A factor which was not important until recently.'

The suspense was killing her, and she watched as he took a generous sip of his liqueur, hating his unruffled calm, the almost ruthless implacability he was able to generate with appalling ease. Little wonder he was considered a diabolical adversary among his competitors; a pitiless, inflexible force as head of his own directorial board.

'Angela has the use of the Darling Point home during her lifetime, and relinquishes occupancy only if she chooses to remarry.' His eyes were devoid of expression. 'Your father made one exception. If you married me, Angela would then inherit the property outright, as well as retaining her generous annuity.'

'I see.' Amazing how composed she sounded when her emotions were warring between intense anger and a sense of outrage.

'There's more,' he revealed drily, watching the tenseness at the edge of her mouth, the faint pallor of her skin. 'Information I'd prefer you to hear from me, rather than as social gossip.' He paused momentarily, taking his time. 'Angela is contemplating marriage, but convention and the terms of your father's will dictate that your future should be decided first.'

She could have screamed at his implacable façade, wanting, *needing* some degree of reassurance, and only acquired poise and willpower kept her voice level. 'I'm expected to agree to an engagement and marry you within a matter of months, thus leaving the way free for my dear stepmother to remarry and inherit a chunk of prime real estate, valued at what——' she hesitated, hazarding '—six million?'

'Seven,' Jared corrected silkily, adding, 'on today's market, including fittings and furniture.'

Kris didn't even blink. 'An amount not to be sneezed at,' she managed coolly, holding his gaze with equanimity as she ventured with unaccustomed dryness, 'somehow I can't imagine you being a pawn in this particular scheme.'

He was silent for so long, she began to wonder if he intended to comment at all.

'My reasons for wanting to marry you are entirely selfish,' he drawled at last, and she forced a tight smile.

'Chayse-Laurensen.'

'You make it sound like a business merger.'

A bitter laugh escaped her throat. 'Don't insult my intelligence by inferring otherwise!'

'Your welfare has always afforded concern,' he declared steadily, and her mouth shook a little as she endeavoured to keep a tight rein on her emotions. If she didn't resort to flippancy she'd burst into ignominious tears.

'Of course. I should be grateful. This elegant mansion is even more prestigious than the home I infrequently occupy. If I agree to marry you, I'll have a husband whose personal wealth exceeds my own, who is socially sought after, and whose reputation with women is legendary. I'll be the envy of every female in the State—if not the entire country.' Kris didn't even waver as the words slipped from her tongue like silver-tipped darts. 'Why, you've even spared me having to give a thought to my future. Doubtless tentative arrangements have already been made, waiting to be put into action. Let me guess,' she paused, tilting her head to one side in apparent contemplation. 'What comes next, Jared? Do you produce a ring of suitable magnificence, release an announcement to the news media, assure me we'll live happily ever after, then bundle me home like an amenable, *sensible* little girl?' A slightly harsh laughed bubbled forth from her lips. 'Angela will, of course, be aware what this evening is all about, and will inevitably confront me first thing tomorrow as to my decision. Imagine what hell will break loose should I tell her I might dare to refuse! The prospect of seeing seven million dollars, plus a generous annuity, slip from her fingers could provoke quite a scene. Tell me, would she have the right to turn me out?'

'You're being overly dramatic.'

'Am I?' Kris queried sadly. 'I'm trying very hard to retain my sanity.'

His measured silence stretched for unbearable moments, until she could stand it no longer, and with a muffled excuse she rose to her feet.

'I'd like to go home.' She felt wretched, almost ill with nervous reaction, and the need to be alone was paramount.

'Come into the lounge and we'll have coffee,' Jared bade brusquely, his eyes narrowing as she shook her head in silent negation.

'I couldn't drink it. Tonight has proved to be an illuminating experience. It might be best if you called me a taxi.' She sounded so weary that she scarcely recognised the voice as her own.

'I'll drive you.' A thread of anger was apparent, silently daring her to thwart him, and she gave a helpless shrug in acquiescence as she collected her evening purse.

In the car she sat in silence, her mind clouded with a complexity of emotions too disjointed to untangle, and she reached for the door-clasp the instant Jared brought the vehicle to a halt in the driveway.

Good manners demanded she issue a polite thanks, and she was totally unprepared as he leant forward and bestowed a brief, hard kiss on her unsuspecting lips.

'Sleep well,' he bade with gentle mockery, and he made no attempt to stop her as she slid out from the car, waiting only long enough for her to enter the house before sending the luxurious vehicle whispering towards the gates.

CHAPTER FOUR

'AH, there you are.'

Kris glanced up from scanning the morning newspaper and cast Angela a careful look over the top of her coffee cup, undecided whether she shouldn't have taken the easy way out and escaped to the beach for the day. Only sheer dogged resolve was responsible for not delaying a confrontation with her stepmother. That, and philosophical resignation. Besides, with fore-knowledge Angela was unlikely to let the matter rest until she knew the outcome.

'I think I'll join you.'

Kris watched as the older woman slid into a chair opposite, and felt very cynical as she waited for Angela to begin.

'Jared spoke to you last night.'

The direct attack, no less. Trust her stepmother not to waste time bandying words! 'Yes.'

'Not very forthcoming, are you, my dear?'

Give me one good reason why I should make it easy for you, Kris upbraided silently, feeling anger begin to surface all over again until she *burned* with it. She wasn't sure which hurt the most—the fact she'd never guessed what they'd had in mind, or that they could imagine she wouldn't provide any resistance.

'It was the element of surprise which caught me unawares,' Kris offered at last, catching Angela's direct gaze and holding it unwaveringly.

'You always did have your head in the clouds. One has to be incredibly astute to take advantage of any opportunity.'

'And marrying Jared fits into that category, of course.'

'Well, darling,' Angela enunciated carefully, elaborating as if she was explaining something terribly important to a rather dense, or at best naïve, child, 'Jared is an extremely wealthy man—attractive, intelligent. You could do no better.'

'You stand to lose a fortune if I refuse.' It wasn't in her nature to be bitchy, but it was one barb she intended to strike home.

'Doesn't it mean anything to you that the terms of Sven's will indicate that he considered it his dearest wish that you and Jared should eventually marry?'

One point to Angela, Kris thought wryly. Taking a deep breath, she ventured slowly, 'Love, of course, doesn't figure in any of these machinations.'

'Good heavens, what has *love* got to do with it?'

'Next, you'll tell me you didn't love my father.' The words slipped out before she could stop them, and a deep pain enveloped her heart as she caught Angela's calculating expression.

'I knew I could make him happy. Isn't that just as important?' The older woman lifted a hand in a gesture that was meant to encompass not only the room, but the entire house. 'In return, I lived among the society I'd always coveted, enjoyed my role as his wife and hostess. I was very fond of your father. Aware,' she added with cool deliberation, 'that I could never take your mother's place.'

I never knew her, Kris reflected sadly. The only record I have of her existence is a number of photographs depicting a beautiful young woman to whom I bear very little resemblance.

'I haven't given Jared an answer,' she declared, looking at Angela squarely, determined not to be bulldozed into anything. For once in her life, the ball was in her court.

'But you will—soon.'

'I need to think about it. Without being pressured,' she added with deliberate emphasis, wondering why the sudden brilliance of her stepmother's smile should niggle away deep in her subconscious, making her feel wary and the victim rather than the victor in their exchange.

'Who would provide any pressure, darling?' Angela queried with a careless shrug. 'Now, what do you have planned for today?'

Nothing, Kris felt like saying, but the thought of spending the day in her stepmother's company was more than she could bear. Instead, she invented the first excuse that came to mind. 'Shopping—I have a few last-minute gifts. Sam can drop me off in the city,' she added carelessly. 'Or if you need him, I'll take the Mercedes.'

'Oh, Sam darling—the traffic will be abominable. Actually, you can do me a favour. I have a few pieces of jewellery at Hardy's which need to be collected. You don't mind, do you? If you leave it until last, Sam can simply double-park outside.'

An hour later Kris decided she must have been mad to suggest shopping as an escape. The streets were crowded, the pavements choked as people vied for space, jostling impatiently as they juggled carrier bags and parcels in the enervating heat. Department stores, boutiques were filled with customers intent on securing their purchases, and shop assistants appeared just as harassed as their clientele.

Seeking temporary respite proved fruitless, for it was midday and every coffee lounge she sought was filled to capacity with weary patrons intent on taking a short rest while sipping something long and cool in a bid to assist temporary revival.

In the end she had to be content with a sandwich and a can of drink in nearby Hyde Park with a number of pigeons hovering nearby, exasperated mothers with tired irritable children, and teenage punks in garish garb.

By three o'clock she had two books, a set of expensive notepaper and an exquisite designer scarf reposing in a large carrier bag. Most of her Christmas gifts had been purchased in Paris— selections which had caused endless deliberation, for what did you choose for a glamorous stepmother who had absolutely everything? Or Jared? Each successive year it became a quest for the unusual, something individual rather than unnecessarily expensive.

Kris entered the exclusive jewellery store with half an hour to spare, glad of its air-conditioned interior as she browsed at will.

'Unable to choose?'

The likelihood of Jared frequenting the same jewellery store while she was there seemed remote, and she said as much, conscious of the exasperation evident in her voice as she queried, 'What are you doing here?'

'The same as you, I imagine,' he answered drily, signalling to the hovering manager that he was not yet ready to be attended to.

'With which particular feminine friend in mind?' Kris enquired a trifle waspishly, then cursed her wayward tongue.

'My, my,' Jared drawled silkily. 'Is it the heat, or have you used up all your allowance?'

It wasn't fair. Attired in a lightweight grey suit, white linen shirt and a blue silk tie, he looked *cool*, indomitable in a compelling sort of way.

'Neither. And I've done all my Christmas shopping,' Kris added, irked that he should think she was dithering over the choice of a gift.

'Good,' he accorded crisply, taking hold of her elbow. 'You can help me select something for Mrs Hadfield.'

Startled, she cast him a quick unguarded glance and caught his wry smile.

'She has a penchant for porcelain ornaments. Lladro,' Jared informed her, steering her towards the appropriate display unit. 'What do you think she would like?'

Standing so close she couldn't help but be aware of him. The elusive tang of his aftershave teased her nostrils, adding to the potent charge of an inherent vitality. Unbidden, her breathing quickened fractionally, and a shivery sensation feathered its way down the length of her spine. Her whole body seemed to possess a will of its own, affecting her senses. Primeval sensuality at its most dangerous, and heightened by the knowledge that he intended marriage. *That* was what had kept her tossing with restless apprehension for much of the night. Having him as a guardian was difficult enough to handle, without considering him as husband and lover. Even *thinking* about it set her nerve-ends tingling, stimulating every sensory pulsebeat until she was conscious of a deep consuming ache.

'Kris?'

Oh God, she'd have to pull herself together, otherwise he'd guess at the state of her emotions, and that would be unbearable. Sweeping him a deliberately cool glance, she even managed a slight frown in apparent concentration.

'You're obviously adding to her collection,' she ventured as she swung her attention back to the display cabinet. 'Perhaps it would be easier if you tell me which items she already has.'

Within five minutes they had narrowed it down to a choice between three equally exquisite figurines, and Jared summoned an assistant, made his selection and completed the purchase.

'Angela's jewellery,' Jared slanted urbanely. 'Shall we collect it now?'

Quite why she should be surprised was beyond her.

'Angela rang and asked me to meet you,' he drawled, 'and explain that she's been unavoidably detained on the other side of the city.' He instructed an assistant to fetch the jewellery, and once out of earshot Kris proffered lightly, 'I see. So you've been sent to my rescue instead.'

'You object?'

'Why should I?' she parried evenly, aware of the slight dryness in his voice. 'Although it probably would have been easier if she'd left a message here. I could have caught a taxi home and saved you the bother.'

'I imagine she was concerned at your having expensive jewellery in your possession, and at this time of year finding a taxi in under half an hour would be a minor miracle.'

'I should be grateful,' she agreed, and glimpsed his wry smile.

'But you're not.'

'Doubtlessly I've taken you away from an important appointment. Your secretary is probably livid at having to soothe some justifiably irate VIP, forcing you to compensate by taking him out to dinner.'

'Ah,' he murmured musingly, and the look he cast her held veiled mockery. 'Perhaps I should insist you join us.'

'I can't,' Kris refused without the slightest regret. 'Angela is dragging me off to yet another party.'

'I know.'

'You do?'

His glance was unaccountably cynical. 'We inevitably receive the same invitations.'

Surely she could invent a headache and not go? The thought of another evening in Jared's company was more than she could bear, and it was as well the assistant returned at that moment.

'I'm sure you can find me a taxi,' Kris ventured some five minutes later as Jared steered her through a maze of people crowding the pavement.

'Possibly. However, I'd prefer to deliver you safely home.' He shot her a dark probing glance, warning softly, 'And don't argue.'

It took ten minutes to reach the tall modern edifice housing Chayse-Laurensen's prestigious offices, and a further fifteen before the Aston Martin beneath Jared's competent hands was able to clear the inner city traffic.

Kris sat in silence, and proffered a polite 'thanks' when the car slid to a halt outside the entrance to her home, then she slipped from the car with her purchases, uncaring that he had switched off the engine and was clearly intent on following her indoors.

Civility alone was responsible for her enquiring if he wanted a drink, and she could have hit him for accepting.

'Whisky?' She crossed to the well-stocked bar, reached for the appropriate decanter, selected a glass, added ice, then poured a generous measure of whisky and topped it with a splash of soda. Into another glass she poured lemon squash, diluted it with iced mineral water, then moved to where he stood.

'*Salute.*' It was a carelessly offered toast, one which he acknowledged with a cynical lift of an eyebrow.

'I have no intention of staying more than a few minutes.'

Kris took a long sip from her glass, appreciative of the refreshing cool liquid as it slid down her throat. If he dared to mention last night, she'd scream! As it was, she effected a slight shrug and said quietly, 'You're always welcome, Jared. I simply assumed I'd taken enough of your time.'

His smile was vaguely sardonic, and she watched as he took a generous swallow of whisky, becoming startlingly aware of a *frisson* of fear feathering her skin. It was uncanny to feel so threatened by the one man in whom she had implicit trust. Whatever it was he wanted, she wasn't ready. Not now, maybe not ever. Yet she had a terrible premonition she was already on a roller-coaster, and there was no way off except where and when he directed.

'Angela has elected that tonight will be as good a time as any for you to meet the man in her life,' Jared informed her slowly.

If he had wanted to jolt her composure, he succeeded. Slowly she raised her eyes to his, holding his gaze unflinchingly.

The thought of facing Angela's fiancé made her feel ill. To try and pretend it didn't matter if he usurped her father's place—worse, to even contemplate her stepmother and a comparative stranger living in this house, sharing these rooms, maybe even sleeping in the same bed as her father had done. It was too much.

'I don't even know his name,' Kris ventured in a sad, almost abstract voice. She felt as if she was dying inside, piece by piece, and at this precise moment she hated Angela, hated Jared even more.

He surveyed her silently for several seconds, watching the expressive play of emotions chase fleetingly across her finely boned features.

'Brad Roberts is a consultant neurologist who travels extensively lecturing in his specialised field. Until recently, he lived in the States.' He paused imperceptibly, and one eyebrow slanted in quizzical query. 'You want me to go on?'

Kris was about to offer a stinging retort when her attention was broken by the sound of voices, and her face became a brilliant mask as her stepmother swept into the lounge.

Angela looked positively breathtaking, and her smile was wide as she glanced from one to the other, assessing and analytical, her eyes far too perceptive for Kris's peace of mind. 'Pour me a drink, Jared. I need one.'

The thought of indulging in polite conversation beneath her stepmother's avid gaze was more than Kris could bear, and with a murmured excuse she turned and left the room.

In the safety of her own suite she quickly stripped and made for the spa-bath, filling it to capacity before turning on the jets and adding her favourite bath oil, then she sat for as long as she dared, emerging to towel herself dry, and with her toilette completed she slipped into fresh underwear and donned a simple cotton frock, tugged a brush through her hair, applied moisturiser, then made her way to the dining-room.

Dinner wasn't the easiest of meals, for Angela was as intent on extracting information as Kris was at withholding it. Consequently it became something of a game, and Kris heaved a sigh of relief when Suzy cleared the last of their plates from the table.

'What time do you want to leave?'

The lightly proffered query brought a faint pursing frown to Angela's brow. 'Eight, darling. Have you decided yet what you'll wear?'

For a moment Kris considered the most outlandish creation in her wardrobe, then instantly discarded it. Conformity and convention had been instilled from an early age, and besides, while not exactly a shrinking violet, she nevertheless preferred not to attract undue attention. 'I really hadn't given it much thought,' she ventured carelessly, unable to keep the slight edge of cynicism from entering her voice as she added, 'it depends whether you'd prefer me to portray youthful innocence, or chic sophistication.'

Angela directed her a cool assessing gaze. 'The choice is yours, of course.'

Of course, Kris echoed silently, knowing she'd been very cleverly put in her place, and in a way that discouraged dormant defiance. Aloud, she declared civilly, 'If you'll excuse me, I'll go and get ready.'

In her room she flung open the deep closet and surveyed the impressive array of clothes hanging from an extensive recessed rack. Meticulously sorted into casual, informal, formal, evening wear, it made for easy selection, and Kris pushed hangers this way and that in an effort to come to some decision. Mixing with the cream of Sydney's society meant that no event was ever informal. It might contrive to appear so, but guests inevitably arrived sporting flawless make-up and expertly coiffured hair, and inevitably attired in exclusive designer gear. At least half of the women would have devoted the entire day to their appearance, and anything less than a polished façade would immediately bring censure.

Damn. If she could, she'd opt out of the entire

affair and elect to cool herself off in the pool, then view television or watch a movie on the video recorder. Anything would be better than mixing among a number of people each equally intent on outdoing the others.

After several minutes she had three dresses from which to make a final choice, and after thoughtful contemplation she settled on the electric-blue silk with a draped bodice, shoestring straps, and soft flowing skirt. Cleverly designed, it was ideal for the heat of summer, necessitating only the minimum of underwear, and in a spurt of recklessness she stripped down to briefs, then stepped into the dress, slipping the thin straps over her shoulders before securing the zip.

White backless high-heeled sandals lent necessary height, and Kris viewed her mirrored reflection with detached satisfaction before moving into the bathroom to attend to her make-up.

Effecting a smooth matt finish required careful application of toned foundation cream, and she followed it with skilful touches of blusher to highlight the delicate facial angles. Next she focused attention on her eyes, blending no fewer than three shades of blue eyeshadow to create the desired effect, then added accent with eyeliner and mascara. Lipstick came last, and she selected a soft blush pink, then coated it with gloss.

Her hair had been expertly cut and shaped, and possessing a natural thickness it merely required a good brush to achieve its smooth bell-like style. Selecting her favourite perfume, she sprayed the atomiser generously over the curves of her breasts, then at each wrist, her ankles, behind each knee, and lastly at her nape.

A quick glance at her watch revealed that it was almost eight, and she crossed into her bedroom, extracted a gold bracelet from her jewellery case and slid it on to her wrist, fastened a diamond pendant round her neck, then attached studs to each earlobe.

One final overall glance in the chevalled mirror revealed a slim, breathtakingly beautiful young woman ready to take on the world; poised, assured and confident.

Kris felt she was viewing a projected image, one far removed from the flesh and blood counterpart filled with a complexity of emotions.

With a faint grimace she collected an evening bag, slipped in a few necessary items, then left the room.

Angela was waiting in the lounge, drink in hand, looking—*stunning*, was the only fitting superlative, Kris admitted reluctantly. Attired in a figure-hugging creation in stark black and white, her stepmother didn't look anywhere near her thirty-eight years.

Kris watched as Angela replaced her glass, then walked forward in a waft of Opium perfume.

'Shall we leave? Sam is waiting out front with the car.'

Kris viewed the scene beyond the tinted windows of the Rolls as it whispered through the streets, and thought it slightly incongruous to be setting out for a party in daylight. The sun was already low in the sky, but with the southern States observing daylight saving the brilliant orb would not slip down beyond the horizon for at least another twenty minutes.

If Sam negotiated the evening traffic successfully and didn't incur any unnecessary delays, they should arrive at their hosts' Seaforth home just as the city became bathed in a hazy pearl-grey dusk, when a million pinpricks of light would spring into life, providing a patterned tracery against a rapidly darkening skyline.

Angela was strangely quiet, seemingly content to bask in her own reflective thoughts, and Kris didn't feel sufficiently charitable to bridge the conversation gap by attempting small talk. Now would have been the perfect time for Angela to acquaint her with Brad Roberts' existence, even offer some background information. The meeting had been carefully staged with a degree of calculation, based on the assumption that faced with a roomful of people Kris would hardly be inclined to make a scene.

At least Jared would be there, although any solence she might derive from his company would undoubtedly give rise to speculation, and the last thing she wanted was to feed directly into Angela's hands.

There were something in the vicinity of thirty people milling in the luxuriously appointed lounge, talking, their subdued chatter pierced from time to time with tinkling feminine laughter.

'Kris! I'd hoped to see you here.'

She turned, drink in hand, to meet Simon's brilliant gaze, and managed a suitable response. Dammit, where was Jared? Or Angela, for that matter! The tension was building up inside her, stretching her already tautened nerves to breaking point.

'Another party—same people, different place. Infinitely boring, and merely a repeat of last year's pre-Christmas festivities,' Simon told her with ill-concealed sufferance, and Kris let one eyebrow arch deliberately.

'Why come, if that's how you feel?' The air-conditioning was blessedly cool, and although she endeavoured to give Simon her undivided attention her eyes kept swivelling towards the door.

'Because the parents expect it. Besides, I have to cement friendships with Dad's business associates.' A sardonic smile lurked in the depths of his pale grey eyes. 'You know the adage about doing more business out of the office than in it.'

He was far too cynical for his years, possessing a grating arrogance that almost bordered on the supercilious. 'Do you always abide by your parents' expectations?' It was an idle query, and she scarcely anticipated his pompous answer.

'I'm their son and heir.' His voice softened with silky determination, making Kris shiver at his cold resolve. 'All I need to achieve is marriage to someone whose wealth and ambitions match mine.'

'Good luck, Simon,' she bade with false sweetness.

'We'd make a good team, Kris. You couldn't lose.'

It was so ludicrous, she had consciously to restrain herself from bursting into laughter. 'Is that a proposal?'

'I'm perfectly serious.'

'No doubt you are,' she said solemnly. 'However, I couldn't possible accept.'

'Why not?'

Poor fellow, he sounded quite belligerent and definitely put out. In his mind he quite obviously viewed her as a coveted prize—her inheritance, at least. 'Because I'm not sure I'm ready to marry,' she said quietly, meeting his narrowed gaze squarely. 'And when I do, it will be to someone who cares about *me*, personally, not merely for the acquisition of a fortune.'

Out of the corner of her eye she caught sight of a familiar dark head, and gave a sigh of relief as it moved into her peripheral vision.

'Fairy tales,' scoffed Simon, emptying the contents of his glass in one long swallow. 'Idealism doesn't exist, only realism.'

'I'll choose to disagree, until proved wrong,' Kris declared lightly, and incurred his slight frown.

'You don't have any ambitions at all?' he brooded, toying with his glass. 'Somehow I thought you might have studied finance with a view to entering the exalted Chayse-Laurensen empire, rather than pursuing an empty existence among the social set. Or maybe,' he paused in reflective speculation, 'your dear stepmother is attempting to stage-manage the ultimate coup.' His eyes flared with glittering cynicism. 'Oh, my dear—I hope not, for your sake. Our Jared is not for the fainthearted to tangle with—in bed, or out of it.'

To confirm or deny it would be equally damning. Fortunately she was saved from having to comment by Jared's arrival.

'Talk of the devil,' Simon murmured, and Kris turned slowly, meeting Jared's intent gaze with studied composure.

It was impossible to discern anything from his expression, and she offered him a slow sweet smile in lieu of a greeting.

'Kris. Simon.' Jared's voice was deliberately mild, yet she detected an edge of steel beneath the velvet-smooth surface, a leashed quality that boded ill for any adversary.

Attired in a dark evening suit, immaculate white linen shirt and matching dark silk tie he looked every inch the wealthy potentate, exuding an animalistic sense of power with chilling ease.

'You'll excuse us, Simon?' drawled Jared, sparing the younger man a brief probing glance.

'Of course.'

Kris felt the light clasp on her elbow and didn't demur as Jared moved leisurely towards the opposite side of the room. A strange tightening inside her stomach magnified into a physical pain, and she swayed slightly, in the grip of precarious sensibilities too numerous to explain as she caught sight of Angela talking to a tall, distinguished-looking man close to the door leading out on to the terrace.

This was the moment she'd been dreading, and for a brief second she considered making an escape, then common sense prevailed.

'Smile,' Jared instructed quietly close to her ear, and she turned slightly to meet his narrowed gaze.

'I really can't.' Yet she *must*. It was there in his eyes, a compelling determination from which she drew strength, so that when they reached Angela she was in control, responsive and outwardly charming as Jared effected the introduction.

'Please call me Brad. Mr Roberts sounds much too formal.'

He didn't add 'now that we're practically family', but the inference was there, and Kris became aware of the cool calculation apparent beneath his smiling appraisal. With detached politeness she stood at Jared's side, listened to their conversation with outward interest, even venturing a few innocuous comments of her own, and she smiled so brilliantly her face ached from the concentrated strain.

Angela appeared at her sparkling best, vivacious and incredibly at ease with the situation, while Kris merely felt wretched, her mind whirling with a series of kaleidoscopic memories that had no place in her future.

At last, after a seemingly interminable length of time Jared made an excuse for the need of a cigarette, and Kris didn't demur when he caught hold of her elbow; she merely walked at his side across the terrace and down into the garden without uttering so much as a word.

She still carried her drink, and with a gesture of recklessness she lifted the glass to her lips and drained the contents in one long swallow.

'I'm almost inclined to extend my sympathy.'

'But you won't,' Kris said dispassionately, staring out across the moon-silvered water. He was hard as stone, and totally invincible. In a way she envied him his protective outer shell; incurred through experience and honed to impenetrability, it was a definite asset.

With calm unhurried movements he extracted a cigarette case and lighter from his jacket pocket, placed a slim tube between his lips and lit it.

'I was beginning to think you weren't going to come.' The words seemed to whisper on the still evening air, sad and infinitely forlorn.

'I had to take an aggrieved associate to dinner, remember?' He exhaled smoke with evident enjoyment, then turned slightly towards her. 'Young Sorrenson appeared quite capable of providing some light relief in my absence.'

She looked up at him, finding it difficult to gauge his mood. In the darkness his features were set in stern relief, their planes outlined briefly whenever he drew on his cigarette.

'Simon is very ambitious.'

'As long as his ambitions don't extend to you,' Jared said drily, and she uttered a hollow laugh.

'He asked me to marry him.'

She felt the intensity of his gaze, and almost swayed beneath it. 'Surprised, Jared?'

'You're a very beautiful young woman.'

'I could have a weight problem, a skin problem, be terribly plain, and he'd still ask me.'

'Cynicism doesn't suit you,' he chided silkily, and she was stung to retort,

'Don't you care that I didn't accept?'

With a careless gesture he threw down the cigarette and crushed it with his shoe. 'Did you want to?'

Oh God, how could he ask that? Simon Sorrenson was a boorish oaf in his own account, and beside Jared he paled into insignificance. 'His reasons are no less mercenary than yours,' she managed after a measurable silence.

'Is that what you think?'

'If I had my way, I wouldn't *think* at all!' she cried, severely tried, aware of a deep-seated rage rising steadily to the surface.

'Do you want to go back?'

With remarkable control Kris met Jared's inscrutable expression, then took a deep breath. She needed to, otherwise she'd explode! 'To the party?' It was the last thing she wanted. 'Will you be shocked if I say no?'

'What else would you suggest?'

'You don't even sound surprised. Why?' she demanded, her eyes furiously alive.

'I've no particular desire to see you become an object of avid speculation.'

'Why—Jared. An *ally*?'

'You see me as your enemy?' he parried smoothly, and she tilted her head in seeming contemplation.

'A master chess player, perhaps,' she conceded, adding silently—Aware of every move, letting me gain a small victory now and again, boosting my confidence, breaking down my defences. Her gaze lifted, her eyes searching his in the night's darkness.

He stood there, silent and compelling, and it seemed an age before he spoke.

'Don't take it into your head to play games with me, Kris,' he cautioned softly. 'Be warned I'll turn any advantage against you and use it without the slightest hesitation.'

She felt her eyes widen momentarily, and she took a quick backwards step as his hands closed over her shoulders. 'Nothing about you would surprise me.'

In seeming slow motion his head began to descend, his breath gently fanning her forehead, and she struggled, pushing against his chest as he brought her close. His lips brushed hers, settling with unerring ease over their delicate curves as he savoured the sensual softness, then as she clenched her teeth he caught hold of her lower lip and pulled it gently, taking it into his mouth and making her gasp with outraged indignation.

Too late she realised her mistake, for the instant her jaw relaxed his mouth moved on hers, demanding, possessive as he invaded the soft inner sweetness to create havoc with her senses.

Hands slid down her back to enfold her close, then his mouth softened fractionally, gentling as he tasted the swollen contours of her lips. Slowly, he traced an evocative path, savouring their fullness in a deliberately flagrant exploration before slipping to caress the delicate hollows at the base of her throat.

Next, he trailed the pulsing cord at the edge of her neck to her earlobe before slipping along the edge of her jaw to reclaim her mouth.

She was melting inside, warmth slowly encompassing her body, sending the blood pulsing through her veins until her entire being became consumed with a deep throbbing awareness.

Unconsciously her limbs pressed into his, and she dimly registered Jared's quick indrawn breath before his mouth hardened, its pressure becoming relentless as he plundered at will, subjecting her to a degree of sensual mastery she had never even dreamed existed.

Kris was unconscious of her own response, aware only of the almost mindless ecstasy that became a beautiful melding of sheer sensation and elusive alchemy.

There was a terrible sense of loss as he gently disentangled her arms and released her, and she swayed slightly, feeling disorientated for a few heartstopping seconds before normalcy returned, and with it came a sense of shock, locking her limbs into immobility. She felt so infinitely fragile that the slightest movement would have sent her crumbling to an ignominious heap at his feet.

She could only look at him, transfixed, and she didn't even blink as he lifted a hand to her hair and brushed a few stray locks back behind her ear.

Gentle fingers lifted her chin, and her lashes swiftly lowered as she felt his fingertips trace the outline of her mouth. Beneath his featherlight touch she was unable to control the slight trembling, and she heard his soft indistinguishable oath.

Somehow she had to pretend it didn't matter, that his kiss was no more shattering than any she'd previously experienced, and pride alone was responsible for the way she slowly let her lashes sweep upwards to focus on a point slightly above his mouth.

'Perhaps I should blame the wine.' It was amazing, but she managed a shaky smile. 'Will you call me a taxi? I'd like to go home.'

Jared was silent for a few seconds, then he said evenly, 'I'll drive you.'

How could he appear so *calm*? 'No, really,' she protested. 'It's not late. You should stay.'

'Don't argue.' It was a softly veiled threat, emotive, and for some reason she shivered.

'I can't go inside.' It was nothing less than the truth. Knowing how she must look, the connotation that would be placed on their joint appearance . . .

'You'll have to,' Jared inferred inflexibly. 'There's no other way to the front driveway except through the house.' He pushed a hand into his trouser pocket and extracted a key-ring. 'My car is parked just inside the gates. Go there and wait for me. I'll make some suitable excuse.'

The insane thing was that no one seemed to notice. She managed to slip through the lounge into the main entrance foyer, and from there she made her way down the steps without incurring so much as a sideways glance.

The car was synonymous with a silent haven, and she quickly unlocked the door and slipped into the passenger seat.

Jared joined her minutes later, and in the semi-darkness it was difficult to determine much from his brief glance as he fired the engine. Once clear of the gates he sent the Aston Martin purring along Seaforth Crescent towards the Spit.

'What is supposed to ail me?' Kris queried wryly. 'Angela is bound to ask.'

He spared her a brief glance before returning his attention to the road ahead. 'A headache,' he inclined drolly, and a dry laugh escaped her lips.

'Dear Jared. Whatever would I do without you?'

'Why not reconcile yourself to the fact that you don't have to?'

It would be so easy, she didn't even have to think about it. Just say *yes*. Except that the words seemed locked in her throat.

Almost blindly she stared directly ahead, barely conscious of anything beyond the windscreen. There was only the man seated within touching distance, his presence a looming magnetic force in the confines of the car's luxurious interior.

Her mouth felt bruised, her lips slightly swollen, and a shaft of pain exploded deep inside at the vivid memory of his kiss. *Kiss*. It had been more like an annihilation of her soul.

It seemed to take forever to reach Darling Point, and Kris had her hand on the doorclasp the instant Jared brought the car to a halt in the curving driveway.

'So anxious to escape?' he drawled, reaching forward to switch off the ignition, and at once a thousand butterflies inside her stomach began to beat their wings in frightened agitation.

If he touched her, she'd break apart. Summoning tremendous effort, she forced herself to look at him, and her voice sounded calm. Amazing, but she even managed to inject a sliver of humour. 'I'd ask you in, but you must be anxious to get back to the party.'

'Wrong,' he corrected, his voice tinged with mockery, and her eyes widened slightly.

She didn't know the time, but it must be almost midnight. Besides, she really did have the beginnings of a headache—auto-suggestion, perhaps, she decided hollowly. But more than anything, she desperately needed to be alone.

He shifted slightly in his seat, reclining an arm against the steering wheel as he leaned towards her, and she sat still, her eyes widening as he lifted a hand and idly traced the length of her jaw.

'Don't,' she whispered in momentary defeat, feeling shaky and ill-equipped to deal with him. Her mouth trembled as he lightly probed its contours, and a familiar quickening of her pulse warred with a dozen differing emotions, the least enviable being the desire to wind her arms around his neck and evoke any degree of passion he chose to bestow.

'Invite me in.'

Her eyes flew even wider at the humorous implication in his voice, and she wrenched her head away from his grasp. 'No!'

'Such vehemence!' he mocked, framing her face with both hands. 'When I wouldn't harm so much as a hair on your beautiful head.'

It wasn't her head she was worried about! 'I don't particularly want to play mouse to your cat—at least, not tonight.'

She could sense his faint smile a few seconds before his lips caressed hers, then she was free.

'Good night, Kris,' he murmured lazily, reaching across to open her door.

She didn't hesitate in her anxiety to escape, and it took only seconds to reach the front door and relative safety.

He waited until she was indoors before restarting the engine, and Kris glimpsed the brilliant blaze of twin tail-lights disappearing down the drive, then he was gone.

CHAPTER FIVE

DELICATE fingers of sunshine probed warmly through the vertical blinds at her window, and Kris reached out a hand for the small bedside clock, then gave a muffled groan as she caught sight of the time.

An hour before it had been dark, verging on dawn, and she had been no closer to sleep then than she had four hours previously when she had first slipped into bed.

Damn Angela, Brad, *Jared*. Each one of them could take the blame for the chaotic thoughts that had insidiously invaded her brain for much of the night.

With an impatient gesture she swept aside the sheet and slid to her feet, stretching her arms high in an effort to dispel the slight stiffness of her limbs. A brief cotton shift did little to mask her slim curves, and she paused momentarily in idle fascination as she caught sight of her mirrored reflection, the firm thrust of her breasts, the small waist tapering down over slim hips.

Possessed of an odd restlessness, she crossed to the bathroom and sluiced her face with cold water, then she cleaned her teeth and tugged a brush through her hair.

Back in her bedroom she extracted satin shorts and a cotton-knit top and donned them, pulled on socks and jogging shoes and fixed a sweatband on to her forehead. Then she made her way to the kitchen, where she poured a glass of orange juice and quickly drank it before slipping quietly out of the side entrance, only to backtrack in order to release the main gates.

The street was empty, and she broke into a running stride, settling into a comfortable rhythm with ease. At this hour of the morning the air was fresh, and there was none of the oppressive summer heat that inevitably shrouded the city prior to midday and rarely lifted until late afternoon.

With no definite destination in mind Kris simply ran for the sheer enjoyment of it, easing her way towards Rushcutter's Bay. There was a pretty scenic park there, and she circled it before steadily retracing her steps to Darling Point, reaching home feeling invigorated, despite the fine sheen of sweat apparent on the surface of her skin.

Suzy was in the kitchen slicing fresh oranges ready for the juice extractor, and Kris gave her a self-effacing grin.

'You're enthusiastic,' the housekeeper declared. 'I thought you'd still be in bed.'

'I've been up for more than an hour,' Kris informed her as she poured herself a glass of water, and her eyes took on a teasing glint. 'What's more, I'm about to change and plunge into the pool.'

'Ah, what it is to be young!' Suzy muttered, *sotto voce*, and Kris wrinkled her nose with impudent humour.

'After breakfast I intend disappearing for most of the day.'

'More shopping?'

'No, I thought I might go to the beach, improve my tan, read a book.' The idea definitely appealed. Besides, if she stayed around the house Angela would be bound to lay claim to a social engagement and drag her along on some pretext or other, and she really didn't want to indulge in polite chatter or be backed into a proverbial corner and have to comment on Brad Roberts.

After half an hour in the pool Kris emerged to dry off before making her way indoors. In her room she stripped off and stepped beneath the shower, taking her time as she shampooed and conditioned her hair.

Breakfast was a slice of toast and a banana, eaten in solitary enjoyment on the terrace, then Kris picked up the keys to the Mercedes and headed east towards Bondi.

It wasn't until she'd parked the car that she remembered she'd left her book on her bedside pedestal. Not that it mattered, there were shops close by where she could easily buy something to read.

The news agency was busy and she browsed, selecting a suitable book and a magazine before crossing to the counter. Tendering money, she was totally unprepared when the sales assistant blurted in breathless excitement, 'I hope you don't mind me asking, but you *are* Kris Laurensen, aren't you?'

Lord, she hadn't realised she was so easily recognisable! 'Well, yes——'

'I thought so. The photograph doesn't really do you justice, you look much prettier in the flesh.' Once started, the young woman seemed unable to stop. 'Jared Chayse is such a *hunk*, isn't he? Oh, I think it's wonderful. You must both be very happy.'

Happy, *wonderful*?

'I suppose it would be terribly presumptuous of me to ask when the wedding will be?'

Like a jigsaw puzzle the pieces suddenly fell into place, and Kris progressed through indignation and rage to cold hard anger in ten seconds flat.

Somehow she managed to keep her voice bland. 'Terribly,' she answered coolly, and barely registered the young woman's disappointment. She didn't even ask which newspaper featured the announcement, electing instead to collect a copy of each publication, then she paid for her purchases and walked back to the car.

With deliberately controlled movements she slid in behind the wheel, closed the door, then began leafing through the numerous pages.

There were photographs, several of them collectively portraying Jared and herself on no fewer than four different occasions during the past week. However, the scoop was contained in the accompanying gossip report, revealing——

'Kris Laurensen was seen leaving an exclusive inner city jewellery establishment yesterday escorted by Jared Chayse. Speculation that the two might be heading towards the altar was confirmed last night, and a formal announcement is expected soon.'

Slowly she closed the pages and placed the papers on to the passenger seat, then she switched on the ignition and drove into the city.

The tall imposing steel and glass structure housing Chayse-Laurensen was merely one of several modern buildings dotting the city's skyline, and Kris parked in the underground car park, then rode the elevator to the floor where Jared's executive offices were housed.

The plush reception area comprised several expensive leather chairs and offered a large selection of business magazines strategically arranged on low glass-topped tables. Kris bypassed them all and made straight for the reception desk.

'Please inform Mr Chayse that Miss Laurensen is waiting.'

The elegantly-attired receptionist reached for the inter-office telephone, and no sooner had she replaced the receiver than another young woman emerged through a side door and indicated that Kris should accompany her to the executive lounge where she could wait until Jared had concluded an important business call.

It didn't help cool her temper to wait fifteen minutes, and she was almost rigid with anger by the time Jared's secretary eventually escorted her into his office.

Kris entered the room, the words she wanted to hurl at him barely held in check, and the instant they were alone she launched into an attack.

'How *dare* you!' Her voice was filled with such fury it came out in a vengeful rush, conveying censure and condemnation.

Jared moved round the side of his desk and leaned against its edge. Attired in a silver-grey tailored suit he looked every inch the directorial magnate, and totally in command. His expression was watchful, even curiously detached, except that she was so irrationally angry she barely registered anything other than his physical presence.

'And *don't*,' she paused, throwing him a malevolent glare, 'insult me by pretending innocence.'

'I take it you've seen this morning's newspapers,' he drawled with deceptive mildness, enraging her further.

'Three of them,' she enlightened bitingly, and her eyes flared with brilliant blue fire. 'Bearing photographs with suitable captions, complete with innuendo and graphic conjecture.' She was so worked up that her slender frame shook with anger. 'I insist you demand they print a retraction.'

He regarded her silently, holding her intent gaze with imperturbability. 'Have you taken journalistic misinterpretation into account?'

'The *hell* it is!' she retaliated heatedly. 'Do you care how *I* feel? Any of you?' Her eyes resembled glittery blue ice. 'It wouldn't surprise me if it wasn't a deliberate leak—by Angela, *you*. For it would hardly be bearable if I were to upset your carefully laid plans and dare to do the unexpected.'

'Such as?'

His amusement was thinly veiled and tinged with sardonic mockery, his attitude that of a superior adult attempting to deal with a fractious child.

'Don't patronise me, Jared,' she declared fiercely. 'I won't have it.'

'I wasn't aware that I was.'

'Yet you're pushing me into a corner—insisting on my compliance through fair means or foul,' Kris responded bitterly, hating him more at this moment than she'd ever thought possible.

'You don't intend to conform meekly, hm?'

She looked at him steadily, meeting and holding his steely gaze. 'Is that what you want in a wife? Someone who runs to do your bidding at the first beckoning crook of your finger?'

'I want a woman at my side whose intelligence rises above the latest fashion trends, with a sincerity I can count on, and who isn't hellbent on spending money faster than I can make it.'

'And bear your children.' It was a statement she didn't expect him to deny.

'Eventually,' he drawled.

'Why must I be their mother?' It was a cry from

the heart, and the temptation to throw something at him was almost irresistible. 'Your track record with women is well-known. Will the many— liaisons,' she added with delicate emphasis, 'die a natural death?'

'You want my avowal of fidelity?'

'Only if you intend to keep it.'

'In return for satisfying my needs?'

Even the mere thought of what that involved brought the tangle of nerves inside her stomach surging into renewed life. Jared in the role of lover wasn't something she dared dwell upon, and sheer bravery was responsible for the way she held his gaze, although her mouth shook a little as she endeavoured to keep a tight rein on her emotions. A number of flippant remarks rose to mind, but she discarded each and every one, electing to maintain a silent neutrality.

'Is it inconceivable that we might find happiness together?'

'Without love?' It was a cry from the heart, and she almost died as the edges of his mouth curved with cynical amusement.

'I have yet to be convinced such an emotion isn't merely an illusion of the mind,' Jared drawled hatefully, and she was sufficiently goaded to retaliate swiftly,

'Poor Jared! It must be terribly difficult for you. At least half of the women you've—used,' she paused fractionally, 'must have hoped they stirred more than mere—lust.'

'I don't intend imparting a résumé,' he indicated silkily, and she met his gaze unblinkingly.

'My social existence has been deadly dull by comparison,' she reminded him with asperity. 'But then the utmost care has been taken to ensure there are no skeletons in my closet.'

'You sound resentful,' drawled Jared, although his eyes lacked humour.

'Perhaps I am. Does that sound ungrateful?'

He was silent for so long she thought he didn't intend to answer.

'By the time you walk out of this door I want your decision,' he insisted with dangerous softness. 'After which I'll either make an appropriate announcement to the Press, or instruct them to print a retraction.'

She felt as if she had suddenly skated on to very thin ice, and sheer bravado was responsible for her agonised query, 'What if I say no?'

'That's your prerogative,' he returned hardily.

A lump rose in her throat and she swallowed it convulsively. Suddenly she was unable to bear the sight of him looming so close, and she rose to her feet and moved to the window, viewing patches of sparkling water, the inner city with its galaxy of artificial lighting, colourful pinpricks interspersed with slashes of neon advertisements.

'Bricks and mortar, stocks, shares and debentures,' Kris recounted stoically. 'The entire composite that is Chayse-Laurensen. My father died for it, felled in one dramatic swoop by a massive heart attack.' She turned slightly to face him, her expression hauntingly serious. 'Is total dedication so damnably important that it should be permitted to dictate my life—*yours*?'

Kris watched with detached fascination as he moved away from the desk and covered the distance between them.

'You see marriage merely as changing reins from parental authority to conjugal submission?' he queried silkily, and she looked at him wordlessly as he took her chin between thumb and forefinger and tilted it towards him.

She was acutely aware of the latent masculinity he exuded, a raw virility she found increasingly daunting in the light of her own inexperience. There had to be a hundred—maybe a thousand women, she corrected wryly, who would positively leap at the chance of becoming Mrs Jared Chayse. That one would ultimately succeed, given her own refusal, was no less shattering than visions of a future with numerous suitors vying for her attention and offering marriage with indecent haste. She had no illusions that Simon Sorrenson was not merely one of many, and she had a shiver of distaste at the thought of fending off unwanted admirers and becoming increasingly more cynical and embittered as the years went by.

'Yes, or no, Kris?'

She closed her eyes momentarily against his intent regard, afraid he might read too much through the shadowy windows of her mind. Hero-worship had taken on a subtle change over the years, to emerge as a deep unswerving passion. Only *love* could fragment her emotions to such an extent. To accept him would be akin to riding a tiger—but anything else was impossible.

Slowly she let her lashes sweep upward. 'It has to be *yes*,' she answered carefully, seeing herself trapped in the darkness of his eyes.

'Such enthusiasm,' Jared mused with an edge of mockery, and she stood transfixed as he lowered his head to hers and brushed his lips across her own in a warm evocative gesture.

Her mouth trembled for an instant before she tore it away, and she rushed heedlessly into speech, uttering the first words that came to mind. 'How long have I got, Jared? A few days before you slip a brilliant diamond on my finger?' There was no stopping once she'd started. 'Then—two months, maybe three, before you add a wedding band?'

'Something like that,' he agreed equably, although his eyes were peculiarly devoid of expression. 'I can't see it will make it any easier if I allow you longer.'

She held his gaze, her eyes remarkably level, and a tinge of weariness entered her voice. 'Probably not.'

A faint smile teased the corner of his mouth, deepening the grooves slashing each cheek. His eyes ran briefly over her bikini top and cotton skirt, and she made a rueful grimace.

'I started out with the intention of spending the day at the beach.'

Pushing back his cuff, he consulted his watch, crossed to his desk and flipped a switch, instructed his secretary to re-schedule a late afternoon appointment, then turned back towards her. 'We'll have dinner together. Be ready at seven.'

There was little else to do but capitulate, and she crossed to the door with the intention of leaving.

Jared reached it first, accompanying her out to reception.

Kris was supremely conscious of him, and just as she was about to step inside the elevator he leaned down and bestowed a brief hard kiss on her unsuspecting mouth.

'Enjoy your day,' he bade mockingly, and a tide of pink coloured her cheeks.

Without a word she entered the elevator, punched the appropriate button, and stood silently as the doors swished shut, relieved to be free of his inimical presence.

CHAPTER SIX

THERE were any number of beaches from which to choose, and without thought Kris headed across the Harbour Bridge to the northern suburbs, bringing the car to a halt almost half an hour later at the southern end of Shell Cove.

Selecting a relatively secluded spot she set up the beach umbrella, then spread out her towel and lay face down to gaze out over the smooth surface of the sea.

It was an escape at best, albeit a temporary one—from Angela, the inevitable barrage of questions followed by an immediate launch into a plethora of plans. A hollow laugh emerged from her throat. Her dear stepmother would be in her element organising first the engagement, then the wedding of the year.

On the subject of questions—Kris had a few to ask of her own, the most pertinent of which being who had tipped off the Press. The more she thought about it, the more she was inclined to blame her glamorous stepmother.

Damn Angela, *Jared*. Between them, they'd managed her life since an early age. Now, they'd settled her future.

The sun's warmth caressed her limbs, inducing languorous inertia, and after half an hour she turned on to her back, slipped sunglasses down over her eyes and picked up her book, sure that she could lose herself in the printed text. A new release by one of her favourite authors, it promised to be an absorbing read, but after a while she closed the covers, cursing her inability to concentrate.

It was hot, and sweat beaded into rivulets and slowly trickled down between her breasts. Even her scalp prickled with dampness, and her skin bore a sheen of moisture. Rising to her feet, she walked down to the sea, and when the water reached her thighs she executed a neat dive into its translucent depths, to surface within seconds feeling refreshed and cool.

It was after two o'clock, and she elected to curtail any further sunbathing for the day. As it was, her skin glowed and she had no desire to invoke harmful after-effects from over-exposure.

She drove to Double Bay, stopping long enough to buy an iced drink, then she made her way home.

Suzy was busy in the kitchen preparing a sumptuous-looking fruit salad, and she merely grinned as Kris picked out a few segments of pineapple and popped them into her mouth.

'Hm, delicious. Strawberries, too.'

'You've caught the sun,' Suzy observed, and Kris wrinkled her nose as she offered a lighthearted response.

'By tomorrow I'll be a beautiful golden brown.'

'A genuine blonde with lovely skin,' Suzy teased, and Kris tilted her head to one side, her blue eyes full of amusement.

'Oh, I'm just genuine through and through, didn't you know?'

'Yes,' the older woman declared sincerely. 'Warm, affectionate and caring.'

Kris blinked quickly to hide the sudden welling at the back of her eyes, and proffered a slow sweet smile. 'If I am, it's mostly thanks to you. Knowing you'd always be here made everything bearable.' It was true, for Suzy and Sam were as near to surrogate parents as she could get, and synonymous with *home*.

She leaned forward and gave Suzy a quick hug before straightening, then she ventured slowly, 'I've agreed to marry Jared.'

Suzy's face acquired a stillness, and a momentary flicker of concern darkened her eyes, then it was gone. 'Are you happy about it?' she queried carefully, and Kris tried for a smile and settled for a shaky substitute.

'Shouldn't I be?'

'You deserve nothing less.'

Kriss felt incapable of uttering so much as a word, and she swallowed the sudden lump that rose up in her throat, conscious of an immeasurable sadness. After several timeless minutes she offered steadily, 'I won't be home for dinner.'

She moved from the room, and heard the front door close, followed immediately by the sound of Angela's clear voice instructing Sam to bring her shopping in from the car.

There was no hope of escape, and Kris decided that if a confrontation was inevitable, why not now? Walking steadily forward, she schooled her features into polite civility.

'Kris, darling, you're home!' As a greeting it effused seeming warmth, but the dark eyes were strangely watchful.

'Yes. I had a lovely day at the beach,' she declared with the utmost care. For once she held the upper hand where her stepmother was concerned, and she intended to savour every second.

'Come into the conservatory and tell me all about it over a cool drink.'

'There's really nothing to tell,' Kris responded

evenly, and gave a light shrug. 'I lay on the sand and read a book, had a quick swim, then drove home.'

'Share a drink with me, anyway, darling.'

'Maybe later.' She lifted a hand to her hair and raked her fingers through its salt-tangled thickness. 'I need a shower.'

Angela pursed her lips. 'Brad is picking me up in half an hour. We're having cocktails with friends.'

It was amazing, but Kris managed a brilliant smile with scarcely any effort at all. 'How nice for you.'

'Kris——'

'I have to rush—a dinner date.' She didn't even pause as she made for the nearby stairs. 'Enjoy yourselves, won't you?'

Moving lithely down to the second level she made straight for her bedroom and once inside she closed the door, then crossed to the bathroom and turned on the shower, stripping off her skirt and bikini in record speed before stepping beneath the warm spray of water.

Kris was ready at seven, looking coolly elegant in a cream cotton designer creation with black accessories. Her make-up was perfect, understated but giving emphasis to her eyes and the generous curve of her mouth. She'd touched her favourite perfume to every conceivable pulsebeat, and when Suzy buzzed her on the house intercom to announce Jared's arrival she responded that perhaps he might like a drink while she finished fixing her hair.

It was all of ten minutes before she entered the lounge, and she crossed to his side, confident beneath his appreciative appraisal.

'Jared. I hope I haven't kept you waiting.' Her smile was seemingly guileless, and a gleam of amusement appeared briefly in his eyes, then it was gone.

'Our reservation isn't until eight.'

His tailoring was impeccable, the ruffled dress-shirt adding a formality to his dark suit. It didn't matter what he wore, he always managed to project the required image with effortless ease.

'Have you chosen a city restaurant, or one hidden away in the suburbs?' Kris queried lightly as she accepted a glass from his hand. Its cool crisp bouquet was pleasing to the palate, a clearly recognisable German import of high repute.

'A small intimate place within five minutes' drive, and famed for its Italian cuisine. After a year in France, I thought you'd appreciate a change,' Jared drawled, replacing his glass on a nearby table.

Thank heavens for alcohol, Kris decided as she took a long swallow. It guaranteed to dull the edges and aid one's confidence, and generally could be relied upon to act as an imaginary prop in times of need—like now.

With mesmerised fascination she watched as he extracted a small box from his jacket pocket, and she only barely suppressed a startled gasp when he sprang open the catch.

Square-cut and utterly splendid, the solitaire diamond rested in the simplest of settings on a tapered gold band. For a few infinitesimal seconds she didn't even draw breath, and she stood as still as a statue when he took the ring and slipped it on to her finger.

'It's beautiful,' she declared simply. 'Thank you.'

His eyes deepened, the tiny lines fanning outwards, and a faint smile tugged the corner of his mouth. 'So—thank me.'

A customary peck on the cheek seemed terribly

inadequate, yet she really didn't possess the courage to offer more. Dutifully she lifted her head, and standing on tiptoe she aimed for the corner of his mouth. Her lips trembled slightly as she felt his hands close over her waist, and her breathing became shallow, the telltale pulse at the base of her throat thudding with increased rapidity as her lashes lowered in protective defence, before slowly flickering open as she forced herself to meet his gaze.

Unbidden, her nerve-ends quivered in sensory anticipation, and her mouth parted as she edged the tip of her tongue over her lower lip in a purely nervous gesture.

Jared's eyes flared briefly, then his mouth closed over hers, becoming insistent and disruptively sensual as he sought her response.

An exquisite shaft of ecstasy exploded deep within, radiating until it encompassed her whole body, and she clung to him unashamedly, exulting in the sheer mastery of his touch.

'Hmn,' Jared murmured huskily as he gently relinquished her lips, noting her bemusement with a narrowed slightly speculative gaze. 'I shall consider myself thanked—and very nicely, too.'

The return to reality was swift, bringing with it a sense of embarrassment. For the space of a few minutes she'd permitted sheer sensation to rule her emotions, aware that it felt incredibly right to be in his arms.

'Finish your wine, then we'll leave.'

It was remarkably easy to take the line of least resistance, and an hour and two glasses of champagne later Kris was quite prepared to consider her engagement to Jared an accomplished fact.

They had progressed through a superb *antipasto*, partaken of a serving of *fettucine* in a delicious mushroom sauce, and had all but finished the veal *scallopini* when they were interrupted by a series of flashbulbs and simultaneously were besieged by a barrage of questions.

Jared handled each and every one with cool urbanity, displaying a façade that would have convinced the most hardened sceptic that the engagement was nothing less than a love-match.

All Kris had to do was smile, and she managed without any effort at all, acting out a part that would be depicted on celluloid and featured in newsprint for several million readers to veiw the following day.

'I haven't even told Angela yet,' she protested the instant they were alone. A faint grimace tugged her lips as she cradled her glass between both hands.

'I'm sure it will come as no surprise,' Jared declared cynically, and she met his dark eyes with unflinching regard.

'Doubtless my dear stepmama will breathe a sigh of relief that all her plans have at last culminated in fruition,' she said evenly. 'I could so easily have refused to conform.'

'Did you want to?'

She arched a delicate eyebrow. 'Rebellion simply for the hell of it?' Now it was her turn to resort to mockery. 'Will you hold it against me if I say *yes*—for as long as it took me to realise that while I might fight Angela, *you* would prove an insurmountable force?'

'Indeed?' His voice held a silky threat that sent shivers of apprehension slithering down the length of her spine. 'I'm not sure I can accept attempted collusion, or condone the hint of coercion,' he added with deceptive softness.

'I've no intention of reneging, Jared,' she

assured him with droll emphasis. 'In fact, I'm terribly grateful to be spared having to deal with a swarm of ardent suitors. Honestly.' The wine must have taken hold of her tongue, for the words just flowed without conscious thought, spilling out with the utmost clarity, her diction perfect. 'Why should I complain? You'll shower me with gifts, provide for my every need, and together we'll appear to be the perfect couple.' Her eyes widened fractionally and she tilted her head to one side. 'Perhaps I should give *you* a ring. Something terribly expensive and equally significant.' She looked faintly brooding. 'And there's my twenty-first in a few weeks' time. What have you and Angela lined up for that? I don't want for a single thing.'

'Not even a car?'

'Good heavens—why didn't I think of that?' Picking up her glass, Kris drained its contents in one elegant swallow. 'Impossible to imagine I might be allowed to choose one for myself. Something functional with racy lines, and one that will befit my expected image.' She held up a hand and ticked off each finger in turn. 'A Ferrari? A Lamborghini?' she queried sardonically. 'I don't suppose you'd consider a humble sedan?'

'I'm tempted to shake you, do you know that?'

'Oh dear!' She pretended to look horrified. 'If you'd contemplate assault before we're married, what on earth will you do afterwards?'

'Conduct a much more subtle punishment,' Jared returned with glittering cynicism.

Kris elected not to pass comment, and declining dessert she bypassed the cheeseboard in favour of coffee laced with liqueur and topped with cream.

'I must be one of Mademoiselle Jacqueline's most successful young ladies,' Kris mused as she sipped the hot aromatic brew with evident enjoyment. 'My future settled so quickly and in such a satisfactory manner. I wonder if I'll set a record.'

'Probably not. I know of at least two young women who were destined for marriage within weeks of leaving the good Mademoiselle's establishment.'

'We were taught so much,' she proffered absently. 'From fine wines as an accompaniment to each selected course, and not only the selection of a composite menu but how to prepared food to Cordon Bleu standard. I can tell the best cutlery, the finest crystal at a glance, arrange bouquets with professional artistry.' She shot him a slightly mocking smile. 'We studied the stock markets, became versed in the value of jewellery, works of art. And then there was *fashion*. I can tell a Lagerfeld from a St Laurent at a glance, and distinguish Chanel from Dior at twenty paces. Ah, but it didn't stop there. It was terribly important to preserve and maintain the body beautiful—from the top of our prestigious heads to the tips of our toes. Workouts—massage, sauna, sport—but only the acceptably élite and totally ladylike, such as aerobics, tennis, skiing, and horseriding, of course. Nothing too sweaty that would ruin our make-up or tousle a hairstyle into disruptive disarray. And we all had to perfect the French language. There was no such luxury as *free* free time,' she finished with more than a modicum of cynicism.

'You considered the year totally unnecessary?'

It had been far from that, but until recently the reason for her being there had been unclear. Perhaps if she'd known, she might have relaxed and enjoyed it more.

'No, of course not,' she assured him quietly. 'I'm very grateful to have had the opportunity.'

Jared drained the remainder of his coffee, then flicked back the cuff of his jacket. 'It's after eleven. Do you want to go on to a nightclub?'

The thought of exchanging this quiet intimate atmosphere for something infinitely more crowded didn't appeal. 'Would you mind if I said no?' The alcohol was beginning to take effect, and she felt rather sleepy.

It had been an enjoyable evening, and she said as much as he brought the car to a halt in the driveway.

The electric lantern above the front door cast a reflected glow, lighting the interior of the car, and Kris sat very still, unsure whether she should lean forward and kiss him, yet strangely reluctant to do so in case the action should be misconstrued.

She was all too aware that she was no longer merely his ward. By her agreeing to marry him their friendship had irretrievably changed, and she felt oddly vulnerable.

'Will I see you tomorrow?'

'I'm afraid not. I'll be tied up all day, but I'll try to get through to you some time during the evening.'

Kris released her seatbelt and reached for the doorclasp, only to pause as Jared's hand closed over her arm. She turned her head to look at him, and her eyes widened into huge glistening pools as he lifted a hand to her chin, tilting it slightly before lowering his mouth down over hers in a featherlight gesture that was faintly teasing, promising much but delivering little.

Then she was free, and she sat frozen into immobility as he brushed his fingers down her cheek, then trailed them gently across her softly parted lips.

'Good night, Kris.'

He sounded vaguely amused, and without a

word she slid out from the car. The instant she was indoors she heard the engine purr into life, and she locked up, then made her way down to her room, unsure whether she felt disappointed or relieved at his restraint.

'Really, darling, we must have a party to celebrate your engagement.'

The circus had already begun, Kris decided wryly. '*No*, Angela. The announcement has been made, the engagement itself is a *fait accompli*, and I'd far prefer to let the entire thing rest in peace.'

They were sharing breakfast on the terrace, and at this relatively early hour the air retained a tranquil hush that was infinitely soothing. Visually pleasant were a number of white-painted urns placed with symmetrical precision along the balustraded edge, flower-filled and providing a vivid splash of colour beneath the dappled sunlight.

'I'll talk to Jared,' declared Angela, looking mildly reproving, and Kris discarded her toast and settled for coffee.

'Do that.'

'Is it necessary to be quite so—terse?'

Oh dear, Angela had never been her closest friend, but neither had she been an enemy. 'Forgive me,' she said solemnly. 'So much has happened in such a short time I've hardly been able to keep abreast of it all.'

Angela reached for the coffee pot and topped up her cup, then she cradled it between both hands and met Kris's steady gaze across the table.

'You're resentful.'

Kris deliberated carefully, then offered with more than a trace of cynicism, '*Resigned*, I think, is a far more accurate description.'

'I've endeavoured to provide you with a stable background over the past ten years.' Angela's eyes were remarkably direct. 'I haven't lacked for admirers, and there have been several proposals of marriage.'

That was true enough, Kris reflected silently. Why, there had been a time during her mid-teens when she had agonised that Angela might be intent on snaring Jared for herself. She could remember that particular summer vacation as clearly as if it was yesterday, feel a resurgence of the terrible injustice of it all, the impotent rage. It had coloured her thinking, affected her manner, and totally ruined her studies for much of the ensuing year. Letters from home had been horribly uninformative, and she'd been extremely polite during breaks between each semester, incredibly relieved to discover Jared purportedly pursuing a number of nubile young lovelies the following summer and since, showing no apparent inclination to settle for any one.

Perhaps there was an element of compassion in Angela's calculations, but it seemed a little too coincidental that she'd waited until now to choose to remarry.

A timely interruption by Suzy with yet another caller requiring Angela on the telephone precluded Kris from having to pursue the conversation, and her request for the use of the car and Angela's sanction was a mere formality.

Kris escaped to her room to change, choosing something light and cool to wear, then she tended to her make-up, collected a bag and headed towards the garage.

Negotiating the city traffic required all her attention, and she seriously doubted one driver's intention to stay with this world after a particularly hair-raising near-collision at a major intersection.

The heat was oppressive with not even the slightest breeze to ease the sun's relentless heat, and it was a considerable relief to complete her shopping and return home.

There were several messages awaiting her, the two most pertinent being from Angela and Jared, the former indicating a number of engagements requiring her stepmother's attention for what remained of the day and most of the evening, and Jared relaying a similar plight with the unlikelihood of being able to phone as promised during the evening.

Not in the least perturbed, Kris decided she'd finish wrapping her Christmas gifts, have a quick swim in the pool, then help Suzy in the kitchen.

Dinner was a light salad, eaten alone, and afterwards she determinedly viewed a series on television, then when it finished she inserted a cassette into the video recorder, poured herself a glass of wine and followed it with another in a short space of time, then retired to her room at eleven, slipping into bed to fall asleep within minutes of her head touching the pillow.

The advent of Christmas appeared little different to preceding years, with gifts distributed after breakfast, a splendidly festive three-course lunch prepared by Suzy and shared with Jared, who upon arrival greeted everyone with a conviviality suitable to the occasion, and bestowed a kiss on Kris's cheek that was little more than brotherly. If she hadn't been wearing his magnificent diamond as proof positive of their betrothal, she could almost believe she had imagined the entire thing.

Brad arrived during the afternoon and stayed for dinner, fitting in with remarkable ease, and any

onlooker would have judged the gathering as
portraying familial contentedness. Certainly Kris
gave the performance of her life, smiling until she
thought her face would ache from sheer effort, and
more than once she caught Jared studying her
brilliantly sparkling features.

Eventually the evening came to a close, and if
Jared's brief kiss and casually murmured 'good
night' seemed unsatisfactory Kris decided she was
infinitely relieved he hadn't subjected her to a
more public display of affection.

This cosy foursome seemed destined to be
repeated, with an appearance the following day at
Randwick racecourse, and it continued into New
Year with increasingly predictable regularity as the
city's social echelon observed a hectic round of
festivities.

Kris and Jared were rarely alone, and although he
was attentive his solicitous behaviour rankled more
than she cared to admit. Expecting him to persuade
her into sharing his bed, she found it something of an
anticlimax when he displayed no such intention.
Conversely she began a campaign of her own,
deliberately playing the part of an adoring fiancée as
she linked her arm through his, let her fingers trail
down his arm or smiled so prettily that he could
hardly fail to be unaware of her ploy.

In a way it was akin to prodding a sleeping
tiger, an element of danger existent in that it was
only a matter of time before he would pounce.

On the morning of her birthday there were a
number of floral tributes, numerous cables and
cards from various friends scattered throughout
Australia and Europe, a pair of gold-rimmed
crystal goblets from Suzy and Sam, a choker of
pearls from Angela. Jared's gift had to be the most
expensive of all, a Porsche Turbo with personalised

number plates.

There was a party, of course. A perfectly splendid occasion, catered to perfection. At Kris's insistence Suzy and Sam had been relieved of any duties and were present as guests.

Being the centre of attention was a heady experience, and attired in an elegant pale blue silk Bruce Oldfield gown Kris played the part of gracious hostess without any effort at all.

It was as she was cutting the elaborate birthday cake that a guest prompted a query as to when they could be expected tō witness the cutting of her wedding cake.

'St Valentine's Day,' Jared replied before she had a chance to respond, and the shock of his announcement almost robbed her of breath.

Why, that was barely three weeks away! She had thought vaguely Easter, never February, and a hundred questions clouded her brain—like how on earth he could expect everything to be organised on time, with invitations, her dress—*everything*? Then an hysterical bubble of laughter rose and died in her throat in the knowledge that with the omnipotent power of wealth anything was possible. But why so soon? Yet conversely, *why not*?

With the movements of an automaton Kris stood at the head of the table while the chef deftly sliced the cake into small pieces, then she took a plate and dutifully passed it among the guests, all the time smiling, even managing to offer the usual inane pleasantries that befitted such an occasion.

There was more champagne offered, and she responded with a pre-rehearsed speech of thanks, then mercifully the shift of attention dissipated as everyone moved into distinct groups and the younger guests slowly drifted out on to the terrace where a disc jockey fronted electronic equipment.

'You haven't sampled your own cake.'

Kris glanced up and caught Jared's dark enigmatic expression, and her eyes widened as she watched him reach out a hand and select a piece of cake from the nearby table. With a strange fascination she followed his actions as he bit into it, then he offered her the remaining morsel, his smile warm and disruptively sensual as he silently cajoled her to take it.

There was a blatant sensuality in sharing his food, an awareness of intended intimacy that sent shockwaves sweeping down the length of her spine.

In desperation she lifted her glass and resolutely sipped its contents, then she stifled a silent gasp when it was removed from her fingers and placed on a nearby table.

'Dance with me.'

She could hardly refuse, and with a sense of mounting panic she followed his unhurried lead towards the adjoining terrace.

As his arms closed round her she stiffened, defensively resisting any intimate contact. 'Do you have to be so convincingly proprietorial?' she demanded in a heated whisper as his hand trailed an exploratory path down the slim curve of her back.

The hard thrust of his thigh against her own brought forth an electrifying awareness, heightening her senses to an alarming degree as she desperately fought to remain calm.

Calm. How could she hope for tranquillity when every nerve-end quivered into vibrant life? She was melting, her body reacting entirely of its own volition as it arched towards his, craving even closer contact, and unbidden her hands reached up to encircle his neck.

Her lips parted, trembling slightly as his head

lowered down to hers, and when his mouth claimed unerring possession she instinctively clung to him, savouring the erotic mastery of his kiss as if it was a lifeline to eternity.

It seemed an age before his lips left hers to trail across her cheek and bury themselves in her hair, and she turned her head into his shoulder in an effort to hide the heated flush she knew must be evident.

Slowly she extricated herself from his arms, becoming aware of her surroundings, the music, guests. For the space of—how long—a few minutes, *several*?—she'd been transported high on to an elusive illusory plateau where logic was an unknown entity and sheer enchantment ruled.

To any observer they must have appeared totally engrossed in each other, and Kris thought hollowly that that was precisely what Jared intended.

God, what a *fool* she was to have momentarily lost sight of reality. An untutored innocent too naïve to tell the difference between deliberate seduction and genuine passion.

'We'd better go inside,' she said with infinite care, and missed his dark gleaming glance.

'Come sailing with me tomorrow.'

She looked at him with pensive contemplation, unsure what motivated the invitation, then she mentally chastised herself. In the past she'd often been a guest aboard his luxury yacht. Motorised and boasting splendid fittings, *Lady* was extremely stylish and the ultimate in pleasure-craft.

'Do you need to think about it?' Jared slanted a trifle cynically, and she weathered his intent scrutiny with unblinking solemnity.

'No, of course not. Will anyone else be on board?'

'Afraid to be alone with me, Kris?' he drawled, and she held his gaze without any problem at all.

'Why should you think that?' she asked evenly, her eyes wide and clear. 'I don't fear you,' she added with quiet dignity, knowing it wasn't so much fear as an inability to cope with her acute awareness of his sexuality.

'I'm relieved to hear it,' he declared dryly.

'What time?'

'Nine.' He took her arm and led her indoors. 'I'll pick you up.'

CHAPTER SEVEN

PORT JACKSON looked incredibly beautiful as *Lady* slid effortlessly through its translucent blue waters. The sun shone brilliantly, pouring down warmth with unstinting generosity, tempered only by a slight breeze blowing in off the Pacific Ocean.

There were several craft afloat, and Jared handled the yacht with an ease born of long practice. Attired in white casual shorts and short-sleeved shirt with espadrilles on his feet, a rakish cap on his head, he looked infinitely relaxed. Even content, Kris added in qualification as she crossed to where he stood behind the controls.

'Are we headed anywhere in particular?'

His glance speared her features, then settled on her bare head with a faint frown. 'Go and get a hat,' he bade, returning his attention directly ahead.

'Yessir.' She made a mock salute and gave him an impudent grin.

'Don't be sassy,' Jared rebuked, and she wrinkled her nose at him.

With very little effort she could imagine this to be last summer, or even one more distant, when they had enjoyed a teasing camaraderie. She had felt safe then, sure of the bounds of their relationship.

'You haven't answered my question,' she reminded him calmly.

'I will, when you've put seomthing on your head.'

She loved the feel of salt spray on her skin, the

sun, and she wore a bikini beneath the thigh-length
cotton-knit top belted loosely at her waist. In a soft
shade of lilac, it highlighted her golden tan and lent
emphasis to the deep sapphire blue of her eyes.
Soon after coming aboard she had slipped her feet
free of sandals, and beside Jared's tall muscled frame
she knew she must appear intensely young.

'Have I suddenly grown horns?'

Kris felt her eyes widen slightly, unaware she
had been guilty of staring. 'No, of course not.'
Without a further word she turned and made her
way down into the cabin, located an attractive
sunshade in a nearby cupboard, then pulling it on
she checked her watch and decided to pour them
both a cool drink. It was still quite early, but it
seemed hours since she'd had orange juice
followed by black coffee.

Jared had brought a packed hamper of food
aboard, and she crossed to the small fridge,
extracted two appetising salad rolls, placed them
on a tray, added the drinks and then made her way
up on deck.

'It must be the sea air, but I'm famished,' she
announced as she moved to stand beside him.
Handing him the drink, she offered a roll, then
picked up her own and bit into it with relish. It
tasted delicious, and on finishing it she thought
longingly of the selection of fruit in the picnic
hamper and barely resisted the temptation to
return for a crisp juicy apple.

'We'll anchor off Palm Beach and spend a few
hours there, okay?'

'Lovely,' Kris agreed at once, for Palm Beach
was an idyllic spot and a long-time favourite. In
summers past Jared had inevitably arranged for
her and a few friends to cruise the harbour with
either himself or a trusted employee at the helm.

Thinking back, he'd always been *there*, his presence constant and steady, her peer and idol, the subject of juvenile fantasies. The few selected fellow boarders who'd been invited home to share her vacation had been eloquent in their envy of her, placing Jared high on a pedestal along with numerous pop and television stars of the moment. In fact, Kris was sure Jared had been the reason for her apparent popularity—certainly her numerous friends had shown far more interest in him than they had in her once each vacation commenced. Any outings with Angela or Sam in attendance were borne with sufferance, and Kris was besieged to employ any number of ruses to have Jared accompany them to the ballet, the Opera House, the theatre; prepared to suffer through the most highbrow cultural performance simply to have Jared as their escort.

He must have been bored stiff, Kris mused on reflection, assuredly amused by their various schoolgirlish conspiracies. Why had he done it? Surely not purely out of a sense of duty? He was, after all, not even related by marriage. Unless, even then, he was intent on securing his future.

The change in engine tempo interrupted her reverie, and she moved slowly away from the railing as Jared prepared to drop anchor. Collecting the tray, she carried it down into the cabin, then picked up her towel, a bottle of sunscreen lotion and a book before making her way back on deck.

Jared had discarded his shirt and was stretched out near the bow, book in hand, his eyes shaded by sunglasses, and he glanced up as she sank down a short distance away.

'Do you want to use some of my lotion?' She extended the bottle, watching as a sudden burst of blue fire exploded from her hand in reflected prismatic shards, and she gazed at the diamond adorning her finger with fascination, mesmerised by its brilliance.

'Thanks.' He applied it over his chest and arms, then passed her the bottle. 'Do my back for me.'

His tone was vaguely indolent, and Kris cast him a cautious glance from beneath long silk-fringed lashes, then she moved to kneel behind him, beginning the task with detached competence.

At least she tried, and for the space of a few seconds she was actually able to convince herself she was immune to the feel of his skin beneath her fingers as she smoothed lotion over the broad expanse of his muscular shoulders.

It was crazy, but she wanted to stroke the outline of well-honed sinew across the boned structure of his frame, trace each vertebra and linger tantalisingly where his rib cage narrowed down towards his waist. There wasn't a spare ounce of flesh in evidence, the result of a strict fitness regime combined with a penchant for tennis and squash.

With determined effort Kris sank back on her heels and recapped the bottle, and was about to rise to her feet when he swung round to face her.

'My turn, hm?'

His smile was without mockery, and Kris remained perfectly still as he retrieved the bottle from her nerveless fingers.

'I can manage the front myself,' she said in a faintly strangled voice as she undid the belt and pulled the cotton top over her head, then she presented her back to him, conscious of the brevity of her bikini beneath his gaze. The twin pieces of white synthetic silk adequately covered her slim curves, and were far from being immodest by present-day standards, nevertheless she felt acutely vulnerable, almost naked as his fingers applied the lotion with firm even strokes.

Her thanks on completion came out as a husky murmur, and she deliberately avoided glancing at him as she moved a few feet distant, then spreading out her towel she lay face down and pretended interest in her book.

Lines danced before her eyes, and she read and re-read the same paragraph innumerable times before managing to gain a measure of concentration.

All too frequently her attention wandered to the man lounging nearby, and she turned pages perfunctorily for the sake of it until she judged it time to change position, then she turned on to her back, covered her face and closed her eyes, only to open them seconds later as a cool blob of lotion landed on her waist.

'Lie still,' drawled Jared, and she froze, the breath catching in her throat as he calmly took care of every visible inch of exposed skin.

His touch was nothing less than a caress, and it required considerable effort to regulate her breathing when every instinct screamed for him to desist. As it was, her stomach muscles tightened, and she could feel her breasts swell, their peaks tautening against the confines of covering silk.

The warmth that began deep within slowly spread until it became a tangible ache, and just as she thought she couldn't bear it any longer he stopped.

'All done.'

She sensed rather than heard him move, and after a few heartstopping seconds she slowly released her breath. Her pulse raced with a crazy tattoo-like beat, and she could actually feel its leap

beneath her skin, *hear* its painful thudding. *Oh God!*
She closed her eyes tightly against the image of his
lips on her skin, and dark wanton thoughts filled
her mind as she envisaged his lovemaking and her
own craven response. Within weeks it would be a
reality, and while part of her hungered with aching
need, the other recoiled with fear of the unknown.
Anticipation of the sexual act was both agony and
ecstasy, a mystery evolving from an elusive
alchemy activated and generated by physical lust.
Yet coloured by love it transcended to the realms
of poetic beauty.

Kris felt as if she was caught up on an
emotional see-saw, at odds with her own inhibitions.
Perhaps she was a prude, after all. Old-fashioned,
and out of step with today's era where promiscuity
was the norm and virginity was something to be
discarded at the earliest possible opportunity.

With a sudden gesture of impatience she rose to
her feet and moved quickly down into the cabin in
search of a cool drink. Icy, she decided cryptically,
selecting a can of orange mineral water from the
fridge. Pulling off the tab, she lifted the can to her
lips and drank almost half its contents in one long
swallow, then she placed it on the bench nearby
and pressed cool fingers to her throbbing temples.

'Too much sun?'

She hadn't heard a sound, and she turned slightly
towards him, her movements carefully controlled as
she reached into the fridge. 'I'll get you a beer. You
must want one. It's awfully hot up there.' She
handed it to him, and watched as he took it from her,
then put it down unopened on the bench.

In the small confines of the cabin he seemed to
loom large, his tall frame silhouetted against the
steps, and with the sun behind him his expression
was difficult to discern.

'Shall I get lunch?' She had to say something, anything to break the electric tension evident, and she turned back to the fridge, retrieving sliced ham, salami, lettuce, tomatoes, some butter for the bread rolls, then she closed the door and reached into a cupboard for plates and cutlery.

When the small table was set she mixed the salad dressing, took a selection of fruit from the hamper, added paper napkins, then glanced somewhere in the vicinity of his shoulder.

'I'll go up and get my top.'

'The sight of your scantily-clad body won't affect my appetite,' Jared drawled, and she forced herself to meet his gaze.

'I didn't imagine it would.' She made to move past him, only to be thwarted in her attmept as he caught hold of her chin between thumb and forefinger and lifted it high.

'Stop it,' he bade brusquely.

Kris felt her eyes widen in silent askance, then she let her lashes flutter down in reflex defence of his glittery gaze. 'I don't know what you're talking about.'

'No?' His breath fanned her forehead, and she could smell the faint tang of cologne mixed with suntan lotion. 'You're as nervous as a kitten.'

That was a mild comparison, she thought wildly, hoping he was unable to fully discern the state of her emotions. 'I'm tired,' she offered in excuse. 'It was almost four before the last guest left, and it's not every night a girl gets to celebrate her twenty-first birthday, or be the recipient of so many beautiful gifts.' Come to think of it, she hadn't done much more than proffer a polite word of thanks for the car. 'The Porsche is far too expensive.' That wasn't what she wanted to say, she thought wretchedly. 'I mean, it's a beautiful car——'

'But you don't like it,' he finished coolly, releasing her chin, and she shook her head in quick negation.

'Of course I like it. Heavens, who wouldn't?' She lifted a hand, then let it fall to her side in helpless resignation. 'I didn't expect anything quite so——' she faltered, then added '—extravagant.'

'You needed a car of your own. I bought you one. It's as simple as that.'

Perhaps it was. But a *Porsche*, and turbo-charged? She would have been equally happy with something that cost a fraction of the price.

'You're—swamping me,' she declared, at a loss to explain her vulnerability.

'In more ways than one.'

She could prevaricate, or go for honesty. Either way she was doomed. 'Yes.'

'Then you'll be relieved to hear I'll be in Perth for a week.'

Her heart lurched sickeningly and began to thud. 'When do you leave?'

'Tomorrow morning.'

How was she supposed to fill her time while he was away? The days were already accounted for with shopping, fittings, and an endless list of things Angela considered essential, but the evenings were something else entirely.

Jared watched the fleeting emotions chase across her expressive features. 'Who knows? You might manage to miss me.'

Without a doubt, she agreed silently. But will you miss me?

'Shall we have lunch?'

Jared's mouth sloped to form a wry smile. 'By all means let's observe convention and eat.'

With adroit sophistication he ensured there were no gaps in their conversation, and Kris began to relax visibly. For a while it was just like old times as she slipped back into a familiar role, and she almost wished it was possible for them to stay the friends they were at this moment. Yet nothing could remain the same, she thought sadly. For better or worse there was no going back. The truth was that she didn't really want to.

The sound of approaching motorcraft wasn't unusual, for Palm Beach was popular with chartered ferry cruises making a daily run from Circular Quay into the nearby Hawkesbury River. Splendid scenery, boating and fishing, together with camping and picnic facilities, made it an enjoyable excursion, and this particular strip of the Pacific Ocean with its numerous beaches and coves carried a flotilla of private craft during the weekend.

A sudden cut in engine noise was followed by a faint thud as another boat came alongside, and Jared uttered a muffled curse as he rose to his feet to investigate.

Kris cleared the table and stacked dishes, then went up on deck to find Jared surrounded by no fewer than three scantily-clad young women, one of whom, she saw with dismay, was Pamela Sloane.

The glamorous model looked absolutely stunning, her bikini so minute that the briefs were little more than a G-string, while the top barely confined her generously curved breasts.

By comparison Kris was aware of her own shortcomings, lack of height being only one, for whereas Pamela was a few inches shorter than Jared, Kris barely reached his shoulder, and Pamela's raven hair flowed down her back like a river of silk to swing at her waist. There were other differences, the most obvious of which was

Pamela's determination to go after whatever she wanted with single-minded resolve. And for years Jared Chayse had been her main objective. Kris had spent a miserable few months in her last year at boarding school when the gossip columns ran hot depicting Pamela as Jared's latest conquest. Then inevitably it had petered out, and another equally beautiful young woman had taken Pamela's place. However, that had never stopped the model from trying, and being in the same social set she managed to attend many of the same parties and functions.

Kris was not sufficiently charitable to imagine Pamela had happened upon them by accident. It was far more likely she'd deliberately instigated a search of the harbour in the hope of sighting *Lady*.

'Why, Kris, you're here, too.' Pamela's smile was dazzling, and Kris offered a polite facsimile in response.

'Yes.' She lifted a hand to her hair in a slightly nervous gesture, becoming aware of the other girls' scrutiny. 'How are you, Pamela?'

'Oh, *fine*.' Her pose was a little false, although her long legs were displayed to perfection as she moved slightly to indicate her friends. 'Sally, Gianna. Kris Laurensen, Jared's newly-acquired fiancée.'

Perhaps there was some hidden meaning in the deliberate emphasis, but Kris didn't attempt to analyse it.

'By the way, when *is* the wedding?' asked Pamela, and when Jared told her she raised her eyebrows in musing speculation. 'Why—heavens, such a short engagement! Somehow I imagined it would be months before you took the plunge.'

'Jared is keen to make an honest woman of me,' Kris declared guilelessly.

'How—intriguing,' drawled Pamela, her assessing glance clearly stating that Jared had to be out of his mind in his choice of prospective wife.

'Darling, aren't you going to ask the girls if they'd like a drink?' The endearment sounded strange on Kris's lips, and the emphasis she accorded it brought a dark gleam to the depths of his eyes.

He must know their presence aboard the yacht was the last thing she wanted! 'I'm sure they must be hot,' she voiced sweetly, letting her eyes sweep slowly from one to the other.

'Let's settle for champers, darling. We have so much to celebrate, after all,' Pamela essayed with a false smile, never for a moment doubting that Jared's bar-fridge might not be fully stocked with anything that took their fancy.

'I'll attend to it,' said Jared, and Kris mentally prepared herself to deal with Pamela in his absence, aware that even the briefest opportunity would not be permitted to escape the model's attempt to subtly denigrate in any possible way.

'Are you flying out with Jared tomorrow?'

'No.' Kris endeavoured to remain calm beneath Pamela's intent gaze. 'It's a business trip.' She effected a light shrug. 'Besides, I have a hundred things to take care of here.'

One eyebrow arched delicately. 'You're very— trusting.' A tinkling laugh emerged from her lips. 'I wouldn't allow Jared out of my sight.'

No, Pamela wouldn't. But then Jared was hardly likely to take any risks before they were married. Afterwards, he might not be quite so careful.

The thought was depressing, as Kris mentally envisaged herself a year from now waiting for him to return home from any number of supposed business dinners, and wondering if his excuse for lateness was bona fide or whether he was sharing time with another woman.

At that moment Jared returned, and when he had opened the champagne she was very careful their fingers didn't touch when she accepted her glass. In fact, she deliberately avoided looking at him at all.

After sipping one glass of the light bubbly liquid she held out her glass for it to be refilled, and sat hugging one knee as she listened idly to the girls' individual attempts at flirting with Jared. She should be used to it after all these years, but the hurt didn't lessen.

How would Jared react if she stood to her feet and ordered Pamela and her friends off the yacht? she pondered darkly. That was what she felt like doing. Yet Jared didn't seem in the least perturbed.

'It's terribly hot, isn't it?'

Kris glanced up at the sound of Pamela's languid voice, then her eyes widened as the other girl calmly undid the shoestring straps of her bikini top and slipped it off to reveal magnificently shaped breasts.

'Ah, that feels better.'

It certainly looked provocative, and Kris stole a circumspect glance in Jared's direction to determine his reaction. He hadn't turned a hair, and she was inclined to wonder if semi-nude sunbathing among his women friends was the norm rather than the exception.

For a moment she was almost inclined to follow suit just to wipe that cynical look off his face, except that it required more daring than she possessed.

'Jared, be an absolute darling and put some sunscreen lotion on my back.' Pamela leant forward and caught the length of her hair together, then coiled it into a twisted knot on top of her head, presenting her beautifully arched back in anticipation of his ministrations.

His smile showed gleaming white teeth as he rose to his feet. 'Sorry, Pamela, I need to fetch more champagne. I'm sure Sally or Gianna will oblige.' He didn't look sorry at all, and Kris glimpsed the model's carefully disguised anger.

'Oh really,' Pamela reproached lightly. 'Kris won't mind.' She swung towards Kris and made a faint moue as Jared disappeared into the cabin.

'Jared and I go back a long way,' Pamela cautioned with deliberate sweetness.

'And I've known him all my life.'

'Ah, but a *ward* is rather different from——'

'A playmate?' Kris interjected, and detected the slight hiss that emerged from between the other girl's perfectly shaped teeth.

The other two girls were watching the exchange with interest, their eyes switching from one to the other as if following a ball tossed back and forth across a tennis net.

'He has several, sweetie,' Pamela stated unequivocally, determined to score a point. 'I often wonder how he ever manages to keep a count of them all.'

'I imagine there were plenty of pretty young things only too ready to throw themselves beneath his feet.' Kris just refrained from saying 'into his bed', but the implication was there, nonetheless.

'I've never noticed him refusing,' Pamela stressed, and her eyes were dark with bitter enmity.

'I think this conversation has gone far enough,

don't you?' Kris managed quietly, unsure whether she could cope with any more. Disparaging invective was detrimental, and inevitably led to a full-scale slanging match if it wasn't held in check. Besides, being bitchy had never been one of her vices.

'Yes. It would be quite dreadful if it was proved your hero has feet of clay.' In one fluid movement Pamela rose to her feet, caught up her bikini top and fastened the ties, then directed Kris a brilliant saccharine smile. 'You'll forgive us if we leave? We want to anchor further inshore and swim.'

At that moment Jared returned, and Kris watched as the girls stepped lithely on to the other boat, their bright smiles and carelessly waving hands rapidly diminishing as the engine spurted to life and roared quickly away.

Somehow she expected Jared to pass comment, and when he didn't she quickly collected the empty glasses and took them down into the small galley, where she rinsed and washed them with unnecessary dedication.

Damn Pamela! She really knew how to unsettle a person, Kris ruminated, disturbed more than she was willing to admit.

'We'll head up the Hawkesbury River and stop off at Patonga or Avalon on the way back for a swim.'

Kris replaced the last glass in the cupboard, neatly folded the teatowel, then turned round to face him.

'You didn't——'

'Come to your rescue?'

She was quietly furious, and it showed in the brightness of her eyes, the deep regulated breathing as she sought for a measure of control.

'You were doing very well on your own,' Jared drawled with hateful cynicism.

'Evading a veritable bevy of highly desirable young socialites, each equally intent on leading you to the altar, must have proved awkward and—*exhausting*.'

'Implying that I take my pleasure whenever offered and rarely discriminate?' There was a hard inflection evident that denoted hidden anger. 'Is that how you see me? An inveterate egotistical rake?'

Kris looked at him carefully and tried to be objective. 'I suppose you're hoping to convince me that your reputation with the opposite sex results from a mixture of conjecture and wishful thinking,' she attributed coolly.

'No.' His eyes narrowed in thoughtful contemplation. 'But to my credit I've ended one association before entering into another, and at no time did I lead any one of them to believe it might conceivably end in marriage.'

'How—practical,' she accorded in an oddly taut voice.

'Realistic.'

'Tell me, Jared, did no one ever turn the tables on you? Not once?' She seemed hell-bent on a path to self-destruction, and could scarcely fathom why.

'No.'

'My, my. You must be very good.' A mischievous imp had hold of her tongue, urging her to say things she'd never dream of uttering, and it was mad—insane, to continue.

'Stop it—*now*,' he warned silkily. 'Or you may very well find out for yourself.'

'Is that a threat or a promise?' What was the matter with her, for heaven's sake? She'd never behaved like this in her life!

'I don't know whether to kiss or spank you—or both,' he drawled, and she became utterly incensed at his condescending tone.

'I'm not a child, dammit!'

'Then stop behaving like one.'

'Maybe I should become a simpering siren,' she rushed on heedlessly. 'And tempt you——'

'To dispense with the bogy of your virginity?' he interrupted with dangerous softness, and Kris felt overcome by the tragedy of it all.

Her eyes resembled huge luminescent pools as she encountered Jared's narrowed gaze. He looked compellingly dynamic, and capable of anything. There was a watchful quality in his stance, a vague ruthlessness that brought her runaway tongue to a faltering halt. To such an extent that she consciously held her breath.

'Is that what you want?' he demanded with deadly softness. 'For me to make love to you?'

No! she wanted to cry out, except that no words emerged from her throat.

He reached out and caught hold of her shoulders, pulling her irresistibly forward.

'Jared——'

His mouth closed over hers, hard and demanding, forcing entry without any effort at all to begin a ravaging exploration that became nothing less than a punishment as he seared the soft inner tissue. It was a brutal invasion of her senses which numbed and shocked, and she was scarcely aware when the pressure eased and took on a persuasive quality.

With feather-lightness he teased the swollen softness of her mouth, then he let his lips drift slowly across her cheekbone to probe the vulnerable hollow beneath her earlobe before trailing steadily down the sensitive cord at her neck to the madly-beating pulse at the base of her throat.

It was like drowning, a slow sinking which she had no will to resist, generating an infinite feeling of helplessness, and almost of its own volition her traitorous body began to respond, melting against him as if drawn by some elusive magnetic pull, and his mouth opened against the sensitised hollow, becoming an erotic instrument as he alternatively teased and probed, creating its own erotic havoc with practised expertise before slipping slowly down to the valley between her breasts.

Kris felt weak and utterly mindless, unaware of anything but the moment, and she made no demur as he slid the ties of her bikini undone.

All her fine body hairs prickled in awareness as his head bent lower, and she gave a tiny gasp as his tongue teased an exploratory circle of one rosy-peaked breast before trailing slowly to render a similar treatment to its twin. It was a lesson in sensual arousal, creating an explosion of ecstacy that spiralled steadily higher until she arched her body closer, and her fingers sought the springy hairs at his nape, unconsciously caressing them as she cradled his head.

An encompassing warmth ran like quicksilver through her veins until her whole body leapt with fire, then his mouth slid up to close over hers in a kiss that consigned anything she had previously experienced into insignificant oblivion.

The earth moved, or maybe it was just the yacht caught in the swell of a passing craft—but *something* was responsible for the strange lifting sensation as she became mindless, lost and locked in a passionate arousal that seemed to know no bounds.

Then suddenly she was free, and she could only look at him dazedly, her lips parting in mute protest, for at that precise moment she felt a desolation so complete it was as if she had suddenly suffered the loss of a limb.

Jared's muttered imprecation brought a soft flood of colour to her cheeks, and she slowly unclasped her hands and let them fall down his arms to rest at her side.

A muscle tensed along his jaw and his eyes darkened until they resembled obsidian chips.

'Please—don't.' Was that her voice? It sounded low and husky, a barely audible murmur that whispered shakily into the stillness of the cabin, and she was powerless to stop the tears that began to well with shimmering brilliance in her eyes.

She sensed rather than heard him move, and felt the light brush of his fingers as they traced the path of her tears.

'You sweet fool,' Jared muttered with wry gentleness, and tilting her chin he slid a hand beneath her hair to hold fast her head, then his lips touched each closed eyelid in turn before slipping to her temple and teasing a downward path to the edge of her quivering mouth. 'What did you think I was going to do? Complete the seduction?' His mouth covered hers, his tongue teasing an evocative path along her lower lip.

'You could,' Kris said sadly, unable to open her eyes, and she felt his lips twist beneath her own.

'Very easily. But afterwards you'd hate yourself—*me*, for taking what you'd only consider to be an unfair advantage.'

A convulsive sob choked in her throat. What he said was true, yet right now she wanted him so badly it was an unbearable torment. 'What do you suggest?' She felt like crying with the futility of it all.

'We go back up on deck and spend what remains of the day exactly as we planned,' he directed, his warm breath invading her mouth.

He stood back, then bent to retrieve her bikini top, handing it to her with a gentle smile.

Kris's fingers shook as she slipped it on, and she couldn't bear to look at him for fear of what she might read in his eyes.

There was a strange feeling of unreality apparent, a bittersweet poignancy in the hours that followed. Especially as the day drew to a close, when Jared delivered her home after an impromptu meal of prawns and calamary eaten al fresco and washed down with chilled white wine.

He brought the car to a halt outside her front door, then leaned an elbow on the steering wheel, his smile warm and infinitely gentle. 'I'll ring you Tuesday evening around seven.'

Kris opted for flippancy. If she didn't, she'd probably burst into tears. 'I'll endeavour to be home.' She released the doorclasp and hastily scrambled to her feet. 'Have a safe flight.'

Then she closed the door and walked into the house without so much as a backward glance.

CHAPTER EIGHT

'DARLING, try not to be *too* difficult, hm?'

Kris looked up from the array of sketches spread out on the table and made an effort not to sound as irritated as she felt. 'Louise is collecting a Bruce Oldfield original in Perth, which takes care of the matron of honour,' she explained patiently, pleased that her friend had not only agreed to accept the invitation, but had willingly acquiesced in the suggested design and colour, thus precluding the necessity of fittings in Sydney.

It was the third day in a row Angela had whisked Kris into an exclusive designer's boutique, and although the choice of wedding gown had been successfully settled, albeit with a few modifications, there were still the co-ordinating colours for the bridal party, bouquets, flowers for the church, a suitable outfit to change into after the wedding—the list was endless.

Perhaps it was just as well Jared was in Perth. Certainly by the time Kris managed to get through each day her energy was almost entirely sapped. Although that wasn't strictly true. Physically, she felt fine. It was the mental trauma of doing battle with Angela over practically everything associated with *the wedding* that proved exasperating. To such an extent that Kris was sorely tempted to ask just whose wedding it was. From the onset she had been determined not to let Angela overrule her regarding a wedding gown, insisting that layers of silk and an immense quantity of intricately patterned French lace fashioned into a demure style of softly-rounded neckline and long sleeves fastened with dozens of tiny pearl buttons were eminently suitable, as were the masses of tulle edged with lace that constituted a veil.

'I'll carry a spray of orchids,' Kris declared decisively, her expression becoming faintly brooding as she deliberated over several sketches and numerous swatches of material. 'A dress to wear away.' She had to choose *something*, although heaven knew where they were headed on their honeymoon. Always assuming they would have one. A tightness manifested itself in the region of her stomach. Damn Jared! He could at least have been more forthcoming. She felt incredibly stupid having to circumvent several queries in the same vein. Inevitably she simply resorted to airy humour and disavowed all knowledge on the grounds that Jared intended it to be a surprise. It seemed the easiest way out.

'Very well, darling,' said Angela, sparing a glance at her watch. 'I think that's it for today.' She offered a conciliatory smile. 'We have half an hour before meeting Sam. I could do with a nice cool drink. We'll have one, shall we?'

A charming coffee lounge nearby offered refuge from the crowded streets, and Kris ordered chilled pineapple juice while Angela settled for iced tea.

'Everything seems to have been centred on me,' Kris ventured idly as she sipped the delicious concoction in its sugar-rimmed glass. 'What about your plans, Angela?'

Her stepmother looked vaguely contemplative. 'Oh, Brad and I thought March. We'll head for Europe, spend several months travelling, and arrive back late spring, I think.'

Kris tried very hard not to let it hurt. Her whole world was changing—irrevocably, she thought

sadly. Yet that was what life was all about.
Nothing could stay the same for ever. Did *all*
brides-to-be feel the same? she agonised. Perhaps.
But most loved the man they were to marry, and
knew themselves loved in return.

Now that the wedding was merely a week distant
she was consumed with nerves, *wanting* to accept all
that Jared offered yet scared witless she wouldn't
measure up to what he expected in bed. Out of it, she
had no doubt she could cope. After all, that was
what she'd been taught—*trained*, she amended with
a faint grimace—to do. It wasn't as if he didn't know
what he was getting, she decided wryly. And that
was something of a disadvantage. Oh *hell*, why did
she feel so insecure? If Jared had once intimated that
love might be a prime factor in their proposed
marriage, she'd be ecstatic. His kisses transported
her heavenward, whereas she had little proof hers
did anything for him! In fact, the more she thought
about it the more vulnerable she became—to a
degree where she could easily cancel everything,
pack a bag and drive north to the Sunshine State,
and thus lose herself in some small backwater town,
never to be found again. Except that Jared would
have someone come after her, or worse, track her
down himself. Somehow the resultant fireworks
were beyond comprehension.

'You're very quiet, Kris. Is something wrong?'

Wrong? Kris almost laughed out loud. What if
she said *yes*? 'Sorry, Angela,' she offered in abject
apology. 'I was lost in thought.' That was true
enough, although her stepmother would be
considerably perturbed if she guessed the nature of
such contemplation!

'Jared will probably phone tonight.'

She tried to look suitably enthusiastic.
'Probably.' He had phoned the previous evening—

a brief, almost businesslike call which lasted mere minutes and left her feeling vaguely bereft and as unsure of him as she'd ever been.

'Shall we leave? It's almost five.'

Once home, Kris made straight for her suite and filled the spa-bath, then relaxed unrepentantly in its gently surging water for half an hour before emerging to towel herself dry. Then, her toilette completed, she donned underwear and selected a pale blue cotton pantsuit from her wardrobe, applied minimum make-up, ran a brush through her hair, and went upstairs to the lounge.

Angela was already there with Brad, looking her usual elegant self in stark black relieved with a clever touch of ivory in the form of a rope of delicately carved beads at her neck and wrist.

'Kris. How are you?' Brad exuded urbane sophistication to the manner born. 'Can I get you a drink?'

It would be churlish to refuse. 'Thank you. Vermouth and soda.' She hadn't known he would be here, and she wondered if they intended dining out. Somehow she didn't feel particularly sociable, although it would never do to hint she'd prefer her own company to theirs.

He crossed to the bar and filled a glass from the concealed fridge, then handed it to her, gesturing a silent salute, and she sipped the contents appreciatively while Angela revealed the day's achievements.

Dinner was an unexpectedly convivial meal, and Kris had almost finished hers when Suzy entered the room to relay that Jared was on the phone.

'I'll take it in the library,' she declared, excusing herself with unhurried ease before making her way to that little-used room near the main entrance hall.

It had been left untouched by redecoration, the one room in the entire house that had been utilised solely by her father. Bookshelves lined each wall, floor to ceiling, and an expensive Turkish rug covered much of the carpet. The antique desk was lovingly cared for, and the leather wingbacked chair beckoned for an occupant as willingly as if Sven himself were there. A last bastion where memories came vividly to mind and the years rolled away like magic, when she was once more a child come to bid her father good night, running to sit on his knee for a lengthy few minutes before being led off to bed by a doting Suzy.

Kris closed the door quietly and crossed to pick up the receiver. 'Jared?'

A faint chuckle came down the line. 'You seem surprised.'

The sound of that deep drawl set up a strange tingling sensation in the pit of her stomach, his image coming to mind without any effort at all, and despite being several thousand kilometres distant she was aware of her quickening pulse.

'I didn't expect you to ring again so soon,' she said.

'No?'

'Is there something wrong?' Impossible to imagine there might be, but she felt inclined to ask.

'Now why should you imagine that?'

His droll query rankled, and she offered sweetly, 'Probably because I find it difficult to believe you've rung merely to enquire about my health.'

'My, my! And I'd hoped you might have noticed my absence,' he quipped with veiled cynicism.

She could quite cheerfully have hit him. '*You* don't have to stand still for hours while a dressmaker pins metres of material into place, then consults with Angela over your head as if you weren't even there!'

'That bad, hm?'

He was amused, damn him! *'Yes.'* Her fingers clenched the receiver in silent resentment. 'I'm sorely tempted to leave them all to it and disappear for a few days.'

'Why not do that?' Jared suggested smoothly, and Kris barely refrained from gasping out loud as she imagined her stepmother's reaction.

'Angela would have a fit! I'd be subjected to a suitable homily on bridal jitters and soothed with words of wisdom pertaining to your eminent suitability as a husband.' Cynicism lent an unaccustomed edge to her voice. 'Besides, where would I go?'

'Why not join me here?'

For a moment she didn't believe she'd heard him correctly.

'Lost for words?'

'Not—exactly,' Kris replied cautiously, sitting straight in the chair as a dozen conflicting thoughts chased through her brain.

'I don't aim to persuade you. A simple yes or no, Kris.'

How could such a decision be *simple*? Joining Jared in Perth could very well be akin to leaping from the proverbial frying pan into the fire!

'Aren't you the slightest bit curious about negotiations affiliated with at least one Chayse-Laurensen deal?'

'An opportunity to see you in action, wheeling and dealing?' she countered, and his husky laugh did strange things to her equilibrium.

'If you like.'

'It sounds intriguing.' Now it was her turn to be amused, although he very neatly took the wind out of her sails seconds later by declaring,

'I'll arrange flight details and have the airline confirm.'

'Hey, I wasn't aware I'd agreed to come,' she protested, and heard his silky rejoinder,

'I'm sure Louise would be delighted. It's more than a year since you've seen each other.'

On that occasion she had been bridesmaid at her friend's wedding. 'She could fly back with me,' Kris said slowly. 'Alan, too, if he can get away.' Enthusiasm gained momentum as Jared's voice confirmed,

'I'll ring them. Now get Angela for me, there's a good girl.'

It was remarkably easy. So much so, that Kris was given to wonder exactly what had transpired between Jared and Angela for her stepmother to agree, relegating various fittings until early next week.

The flying hours between Sydney and Perth were uneventful, the large jet carrying the usual mix of passengers, and on arrival Kris collected her bag, then caught a taxi to Jared's hotel.

It was years since her last visit, and the changes were noticeable, in some cases quite dramatic. A beautiful city, situated several kilometres inland on the meandering expanse of the Swan River, Perth resembled an oasis, reached after traversing some two thousand-odd kilometres of desert country separating the eastern States from the west. Desert that could lie parched for years, then become a magical floral carpet after life-giving rain.

The city itself was a busy central hub which gained much from having its bustling port at Fremantle, the harbour entrance to the vast Indian Ocean.

The hotel was close to Kings Park, its upper floors giving a magnificent view across the river encompassing both western and southern suburbs as well as most of the city.

At first Kris thought the suite was a single one, but there were two bedrooms instead of the one she expected, and a quick glance inside the first revealed masculine possessions in evidence that could only belong to Jared.

A strange hollow feeling manifested itself in the region of her chest, then dispersed as she moved into the second bedroom and began to unpack, determinedly ignoring a faint stirring of unease.

Don't be stupid, she admonished herself silently. There are any number of reasons for sharing a suite.

Name them, an inner voice demanded as she shook out a variety of day and evening wear, placed them one by one on to hangers and put them in the wardrobe.

Perhaps there weren't two single suites vacant on the same floor, although in a hotel this size it seemed unlikely, she decided as she slid underwear into a nearby drawer.

Why should it bother her whether or not Jared anticipated their wedding night? These were the 'eighties, after all. Now or next week—what was the difference?

Damn, she cursed with a husky sigh. She'd been so anxious to have a few days' freedom she hadn't even *thought* what fleeing to Jared's side might involve. Well, she was here now; flying back to Sydney would only serve to compound her actions as those of a capricious fool.

Quite the most sensible thing to do woud be to ring Louise, which she immediately did, and after more than an hour on the phone she felt considerably reassured by the prospect of spending the next day in her friend's company, cheered to learn Jared had already extended an invitation for Louise and Alan to join them for dinner the following evening.

After that she took a long leisurely shower, selected a softly pleated dress in pale florals, teamed it with white high-heeled shoes, then began applying her make-up with care.

In the lounge she moved to the television set and turned it on, switching channels until she found something sufficiently absorbing to watch, then sank down into a nearby chair.

It was after five, and she'd checked her watch no fewer than five times in twice as many minutes, wondering when Jared would put in an appearance.

Just then a key grated in the lock, and she stood momentarily transfixed as the door swung inwards to reveal Jared in its aperture, then he was inside the room, the door closing behind him, and she ventured a slow smile as he moved towards her.

'I was about to fix myself a drink. Shall I get you one?' Amazing she could sound so cool and in control when her stomach was reacting as if a hundred butterflies had just awoken in confinement and were beating their wings in silent protest.

'Whisky, ice, a splash of soda,' he said, his eyes inscrutable despite the faint smile tugging the edge of his mouth.

Would he kiss her? She wanted him to, quite badly.

'Good flight?' He loosened his tie and undid the top button of his pale blue shirt before thrusting one hand into his trouser pocket.

Standing there he resembled a superb jungle cat about to prowl, but with what intent Kris had yet to fathom. Eventually there must come the day when she would no longer be in awe of him, but now she viewed him warily, covering her own contrary emotions with outward ease as she poured his whisky and fixed a Perrier spiked with vodka for herself.

'Yes. I called Suzy to let her know I'd arrived safely, had a long chat with Louise, unpacked, took a shower.'

'We'll eat out,' Jared declared as she handed him the tumbler of whisky. 'I've booked a table for seven. As soon as I've had this, I'll take a shower, then change, and we'll go.'

Kris took a slow sip of her drink and looked at him beneath the thick fringe of her eyelashes. 'You look——' she searched for the right word and came up with '—tired.'

His mouth twisted into a wry grimace and his shoulders lifted in a light shrugging gesture. 'It's been a difficult day. We've been held up with telexed information not arriving on time, the interpreter provided by the agency had to leave abruptly just after lunch due to some acute family emergency, and another interpreter was unprocurable at such short notice. I can't converse in Japanese to any great degree, and my Japanese colleague understood very little English.' One eyebrow lifted with ill-concealed mockery. 'I had to put through a call to New York at midnight last night and was held up for almost two hours before I could make contact. Does that give you some indication?'

'Why not cancel dinner and order room service?' she suggested quietly. 'I don't mind if we don't go out.'

'You didn't come here to sit in a hotel suite,' he drawled, and she shook her head slightly, becoming aware of the tiny lines fanning out from the corners of his eyes, the vague frown creasing his brow, and the distinctly jaded air apparent.

Her eyes deepened with genuine concern and a need to convince him she was sincere. 'Honestly, I'd be just as happy to eat here, watch some television, then have an early night. You don't need to entertain me.'

His piercing regard seemed to sear right through to her soul, and she couldn't have looked away if her life depended on it. 'In that case, we'll take a raincheck and eat in.'

For some unknown reason Kris suddenly became conscious of every breath she took, and the need to regulate each one with extreme care so that he wouldn't guess at the tenuous state of her emotions.

'Would you like me to cancel? I can make the call while you shower.'

Jared's lips twitched in sardonic humour. 'Trying to mother me, Kris?'

She felt immeasurably hurt. 'No, of course not.'

'I'm behaving like a bear,' he dismissed wryly, running a finger round the inside of his shirt collar, loosening it, then he tossed down the contents of his glass in one long swallow.

'More like a disgruntled lion,' she corrected, and glimpsed his gleam of amusement.

'While you were all set on being a ministering angel and soothing my furrowed brow, eh?' He set down his glass, shrugged out of his jacket and hooked it over one shoulder. 'The name of the restaurant is written on a pad beside the phone.' He began walking towards his bedroom, then he turned to offer her a slow warm smile. 'I'll leave everything in your capable hands.'

Her stomach flipped and began a series of crazy somersaults, refusing to settle down until long after she'd cancelled the booking, perused and ordered from the room service menu, then finished her drink.

She was almost inclined to have another, but decided in favour of a Perrier instead, sipping it slowly as she took in the news on television, becoming absorbed to such an extent she failed to hear Jared's return.

'That looks exceedingly grim.'

Kris started at the sound of his voice and flicked him a quick glance. 'It is.' News footage was intensely graphic, and she wondered how the media representative managed to keep his camera rolling and escape injury. Then the segment finished and the newsreader moved on to the day's weather details.

'I've ordered seafood,' she told him as she turned towards him. 'It should be here soon.'

He had changed into casual black cords with a white shirt left unbuttoned at the neck, and his hair was damp, its dark thickness curling at the edge of his nape. He looked refreshed, and the faint muskiness of his aftershave teased her nostrils, heightening her awareness of him.

'Thank you.' He lifted a hand and trailed gentle fingers down the length of her jaw, then he leaned forward and brushed her lips with his own in a tantalising evocative gesture that left her feeling vaguely bereft.

She could only stand there, her eyes widening as he cupped her face with both hands, trying not to lower her lashes in defence as he absently traced each cheekbone with his thumb. His mouth held a faint smile, his eyes dark with a mesmeric warmth in which she could easily drown.

'For what?' If she didn't inject some humour into the situation, it could rapidly get out of hand. 'Ordering dinner?'

Laughter gleamed from those dark depths and he gave a husky laugh. 'That, too.'

A loud double knock at the door heralded the arrival of their meal, and after setting out the various dishes and uncorking the wine, the waiter discreetly left them to enjoy the succulent honey prawns in a bed of rice followed by lobster mornay, a garden salad and an abundance of garlic bread.

Washed down with chilled white wine, it was one of the most enjoyable meals Kris had had for some time, and she sat back replete, her eyes slumbrous and mysterious from the effects of the wine.

'Shall I make coffee?'

'Please. Black, no sugar.'

It took only minutes to boil the kettle and spoon instant coffee into two mugs, then she carried them into the lounge and took a chair a short distance from his.

The main overhead light had been extinguished in favour of two wall-lights, and the television was tuned to a popular comedy series.

Kris watched it with increasing absorption as she sipped her coffee, and it wasn't until the credits rolled that she looked across at Jared.

He was asleep, his head resting against the back of the chair, and her eyes feasted on his strong profile, relaxed and unguarded in repose. Strange, but she hadn't really noticed what thick lashes he had; they were quite long and curled ever so slightly at the tips. From this short distance his legs seemed to stretch out for ever, and she could glimpse a mat of springy dark hair where the shirt parted at his chest.

Should she disturb him? If she didn't, he'd probably stay there for hours, then wake with stiff aching limbs.

Perhaps he might stir if she collected the coffee

mugs and rinsed them, then gathered the dishes and stacked them on to a tray. Moving carefully, she completed the few tasks and placed the loaded tray in the hallway ready for the maid to collect, then locked the outer door.

Jared was still asleep, and she switched off the television, then crossed to his chair with the intention of waking him.

Motivated by some inner compulsion, she lifted her hand and trailed it gently across his thick well-groomed hair. It felt strong and vital, like the man himself, and she stroked its length to his neck. Even as she watched a spasm flickered down the strong jawline, and she traced it with the tips of her fingers, then when he failed to rouse she moved behind his chair and gently massaged the taut muscles, her fingers tactile sensory probes as they sought out the tenseness evident.

He possessed a beautifully shaped head, and after a slight hesitation she slid her fingers through his hair, gently effecting a scalp massage before slipping to rest over each temple.

'Don't stop.'

She almost died at the sound of his voice, and she was powerless to prevent the faint gasp that emerged from her lips. 'I thought you were asleep.'

'I was,' Jared declared huskily, his eyes still closed.

As if scalded Kris snatched her hands back to her sides, and heard his faint sigh.

'I—it's——' She was going to say it was late, but had they dined out they'd probably still be lingering over coffee and liqueurs. 'I think I'll go to bed,' she said at last, only to hear his drawled response,

'Now there's an evocative thought. Yours or mine?'

Her heartbeat seemed to trip before resuming again at a greatly increased speed, its beat so loud she was sure he must hear it. 'Is that why you suggested I come here?' she ventured carefully, feeling very much as if she was treading eggshells.

There was a measurable silence, during which she hardly dared breathe, then his voice razed like finely-honed steel through silk in the stillness of the room.

'Go to bed, Kris. And rest easy,' he added with hateful cynicism. 'I don't sleepwalk.'

Her hands unconsciously clenched into a tight ball, and she turned away and walked towards her room, unable to trust herself to utter a single word.

With the door closed behind her she moved to the bed, turned back the covers, then slowly took off her clothes and donned a cotton nightshirt. In the bathroom she scrubbed her face clean of make-up, switched off the light, then slid between the sheets to lie motionless for what seemed like hours before sinking into merciful somnolence.

CHAPTER NINE

KRIS woke to the sound of the phone's insistent burr, and she blinked off the veils of sleep as she reached for the receiver, slithering into a half-sitting position and sweeping hair off her face in an unconsciously graceful geature.

'Hello?' What time was it, for heaven's sake? Her eyes registered bright sunlight filtering between the vertical blinds.

'Miss Laurensen? This is a wake-up call. It is eight o'clock and your breakfast has been ordered for eight-thirty.'

'Thank you.' She replaced the receiver on the handset and slid out of bed. There was a note propped against the mirrored dressing-table, and she snatched it up, her eyes skimming the powerful scrawl with considerable speed before screwing the paper into a ball and aiming it for the nearby wastepaper bin.

Damn Jared! He'd calmly showered, dressed and breakfasted while she'd slept, penned a note explaining his absence for most of the day, walked into her room unannounced, then arranged a wake-up call when he could easily have woken her himself. Not, she assured herself, that she'd wanted to share his morning meal.

Oh, *hell*. She didn't seem to know what she wanted any more, she decided crossly as she showered and changed into a pale lemon-yellow frock. After picking at the contents on her breakfast tray, she poured strong black coffee into a cup and drank it, then crossed to the bathroom to attend to her make-up.

Louise was to meet her in the downstairs foyer at nine, and she was there waiting when Kris stepped out of the elevator.

'It's so good to see you!'

They both spoke at once, laughed, then hugged each other before standing back.

'You look terrific! Marriage obviously agrees with you,' grimed Kris as she tucked her hand through Louise's elbow.

'*Yes*. I can recommend it.' Louise's dark eyes sparkled with impish humour. 'Let's go, shall we? We've so much catching up to do. Oh, I'm so glad you decided to come. I couldn't believe it when Jared rang and said you were joining him here.'

They walked out on to the street and took a taxi to the Mall, where they wandered talking non-stop through the various arcades, pausing briefly when a boutique took Kris's eye, or Louise insisted that something warranted their attention.

'He's super, isn't he?'

'Who?' Kris looked up from studying the menu and met her friend's faintly shocked gaze, then realisation dawned and she looked suitably contrite. 'Jared? Yes, of course.'

'Just—yes, of course!' Louise repeated in a subdued shriek. 'Good Lord—man's ultimate answer to a maiden's prayer, and you toss him off like that?'

'What do you want me to do? *Swoon?*' Her smile was deliberately wide, but it didn't reach her eyes.

'*Kris!* He's fantastic, and you know it. Hell,' Louise added with a rueful grimace, 'don't you remember how the girls all fought to form a line for an invitation between semesters?'

'Even you?'

'Hah! I never stood a chance. Besides, Alan was waiting in the wings, and I—kind of liked him.'

Kris closed the menu and placed it on the table. 'You didn't mind being steered into a suitable marriage?' she queried with contrived casualness.

'I guess I did, at first,' Louise answered slowly. 'The parents were terrified I'd run off with a penniless wimp, or a smooth playboy whose main skill in life was filching some rich girl's fortune.' Her eyes assumed a shrewdness far beyond her years. 'It's just as much a pain being born rich as it is being born poor. Although the poor wouldn't agree with me!' She laughed, then sobered slightly. 'So—am I to assume this flight into Jared's arms isn't motivated by lust?' When Kris didn't answer she ventured carefully, 'You love him, Kris. You always have. And he rarely let you out of his sight. So, what's the problem?'

The waiter took their order, brought them each a cool drink, then disappeared out of sight.

'That's a laugh. This is the first time *ever* that I've lived at home for more than nine weeks on end.'

'And you haven't figured out why?'

'Oh yes. Chayse-Laurensen.'

'Really? And I thought you were smart.'

'So I'm dumb, blind—stupid.'

'To believe in love? Never. But to refuse to see it when it's right beneath your nose is just plain ridiculous.'

'Indeed?' Kris enquired with delicate cynicism.

'Dear sweet girl—*I* have seen the way Jared looks at you when he's thought no one else was around.' Louise's gaze became intent. 'Remember my wedding? When the car you were travelling in with the best man got a puncture and you arrived late?' She smiled mistily, then broke into a delighted grin. 'Heavens, I thought Jared would tear the place apart! The director of the hired fleet of bridal cars almost developed an ulcer on the spot.'

'He was merely being protective of his ewe lamb.'

'If you believe that, you're a fool. And you're not.'

'What if you're wrong?'

'Oh, *Kris!*' Louise groaned in despair. 'What can I say to make you believe me?'

'Nothing,' Kris responded quietly, adding with a haunting sadness, 'nothing at all.'

Their food arrived, and they ate the ham and salad with enjoyment, declined dessert, and settled for iced coffee.

Afterwards they explored the arcades, window-shopping, talking—but Kris didn't mention Jared again, and Louise very wisely kept her own counsel.

It was almost five when Kris arrived at the hotel, and she inserted her key into the door only to have it opened from the inside by Jared.

'Enjoy your day?'

'Yes. It was terrific to see Louise again.' She moved into the lounge and sank into a nearby chair.

'No purchases?' Jared drawled lazily as he crossed to the bar-fridge and poured her a drink.

'Only one,' Kris informed him as she accepted a tall glass filled with something refreshingly cool.

'We're to meet downstairs in the bar at seven. Alan has booked a table somewhere, he insists we're to be his guests.'

'That's nice.' She was being so polite it was almost ludicrous. 'Was your business meeting successful, or shouldn't I ask?'

'Moderately so.' A faint smile twisted the edges of his mouth. 'At least the interpreter put in an appearance. With a bit of luck Monday will tie it all in and I can fly back with you Tuesday morning.'

'You mean tomorrow is a free day?'

'Surprised?' His teeth gleamed through an amused smile, and she surveyed him carefully,

'You work too hard.'

'Success breeds success—by whatever measure. And that means results equal to, if not better than, the year before. Rather like a ladder. You have to constantly strive to maintain a steady climb.'

'What happens when you reach the top?' Kris asked idly, and incurred his dark slanting glance.

'That's the most difficult position of all.'

'Why?'

'Because you must fight to stay there,' Jared revealed.

'Don't you ever get tired of it all?'

He swirled the contents of his glass, watching as the ice cubes chinked together, then he took a long appreciative swallow and cast her a ruminative look. 'I take a certain pride in continuing in my father's footsteps, developing his concepts, ensuring they reach fruition and ultimately succeed. It becomes a challenge, the people I deal with rather like pieces on a chessboard.'

'Whom you manipulate at will,' she accorded matter-of-factly, and saw his expression harden slightly.

'It works both ways.'

She looked at him carefully. 'I doubt if you would allow anyone to manipulate you—under any circumstance.'

His gaze didn't falter. 'I do—occasionally.'

'Lose a battle in order to win the war?'

'Something like that.'

'Do you apply that sort of strategy to our relationship?' She should never have asked, but having done so she couldn't retract, and his features became an inscrutable mask.

'What makes you think that?'

His silky rejoinder sent icy fingers slithering down her spine.

'You can't answer a question by asking another,' Kris fielded steadily as she replaced her glass. She felt sickened and not a little disillusioned, at odds with herself, Jared. 'I need to shower and change.' Rising to her feet she moved determinedly past him, and had almost reached her door when his voice reached her, and it was full of taunting amusement.

'One day you won't run away.'

Slowly she turned to face him, her gaze remarkably steady. 'Maybe not. But I won't play into your hands and argue. That's what you want, isn't it?' With that she swung back towards her room, and on entering it she carefully closed the door behind her, feeling emotionally electrified and as nervous as a cat on hot bricks.

Kris emerged an hour later, content in the knowledge that she looked her sophisticated best. It was like a veneer, an impenetrable shield one erected in protection. Everything about her was impeccable, from the tips of her Charles Jourdan-clad feet to the top of her immaculately styled hair. A white silk pantsuit with blouson top provided a startling contrast for the black silk jacket. Black shoes with matching evening purse completed the outfit. Diamond studs adorned her ears and were complemented by a diamond teardrop suspended on a slim gold chain at her neck, the finishing touch a gold linked bracelet worn at her wrist.

'Enchanting,' drawled Jared as she walked into the centre of the lounge, and she directed him a slow considering look.

'I haven't deliberately set out to impress.'

'The end result is quite startling.'

It was difficult to determine whether he was sincere, or merely resorting to mockery. 'Thank you,' she said coolly, regarding him with unblinking solemnity as he moved slowly towards her.

'Fix these cufflinks for me, they're the only pair I packed, and I think they might be too big.'

Kris looked at her long, manicured, freshly lacquered nails and gave a slight grimace. 'I doubt I'll be of much help.'

'Try.' He dropped the cufflinks into her hand and extended one wrist.

She managed after several attempts, and stood back as soon as the task was completed, all too aware of the effect his proximity was having on her nervous system.

'I'll get my jacket, then we'll go.' He caught it up from a nearby chair and shrugged it on, then walked towards the door, waiting for her to precede him into the hallway before locking up and pocketing the key.

In the elevator she was intensely aware of him, and felt immeasurably glad when it slid to a halt at ground level, relieved to find Louise and Alan already waiting for them in an adjoining bar.

After that it was relatively easy to slip into another skin and play an expected part. Certainly she smiled a lot, beautifully on several occasions, she was sure, and after her second drink it no longer took too much effort to maintain the façade. Jared was superb in the role of fiancé, and if Kris hadn't known differently, she would have been completely dazzled by his attention. The light touch of his hand at her elbow, the warmth evident in his eyes whenever he looked at her implied a shared intimacy, a secret promise lovers exchanged, and after dinner, when he led her on to the dance floor, she simply melted into his arms, sure that it was totally impossible to do anything else. When his lips brushed her temple she closed her eyes, and while part of her deplored her own duplicity the remaining part fervently wished it was for real.

He held her close, his hands linked at the base of her spine, and she had to physically restrain herself from lifting her head to his, inviting his kiss with a growing need that manifested itself deep within. Like this she could almost believe they were the only two people in the room, the *world*. Nothing else was important; Angela, Chayse-Laurensen didn't exist.

Eventually it was time to leave, and she bade Louise and Alan a whispered good night as she slid out from their car, and didn't offer so much as a word as the elevator transported them swiftly to their appointed floor.

She'd had too much to drink, that was the problem, she decided through a dreamy haze, yet it was rather nice, this floaty feeling. She felt weightless, and then giggled deliciously as she realised she was floating, almost literally, in Jared's arms as he carried her into their suite.

'Oh dear,' Kris murmured huskily. 'Are you going to put me to bed?'

'Will you mind?' His voice sounded dry and vaguely mocking.

'Probably. In the morning.' Her voice sounded as if it came from a distance, and she didn't protest as he slid the silk jacket, then the pantsuit, from her slim form. Then she was lying between the sheets, and the last thing she remembered was his smile. It seemed to invade her dreams, weaving a magic all its own, and when she woke it was a tangible entity, although the evening suit had been replaced by dark cords and a cream short-sleeved shirt.

'Coffee, or orange juice?'

Kris closed her eyes, then opened them again—slowly. She felt terrible. At least her stomach belonged to her, but she had reservations about her head, for as soon as she lifted it from the pillow it ached. 'Both—I think.'

'You'll feel better when you've had a shower and something to eat.'

Callous brute! she thought silently. How come he looked so damned *good*? 'I think I'll go back to sleep.' Another few hours would be heavenly.

'We're spending the day with Louise and Alan,' Jared drawled. 'They're picking us up in an hour. You haven't forgotten, surely?'

Oh, *hell*. Alan was flying them to visit Louise's parents' cattle station east of York. An audible groan left her lips. 'I'll never make it.'

'Yes, you will.'

He sounded amused, darn him. 'You could at least appear sympathetic!' She slid into a sitting position, then gasped out loud and pulled the sheet up to her chin. 'You—took off my clothes?'

'You don't remember?'

'If I did, I wouldn't ask!' The thought of his hands on her body, touching her, brought forth a flood of resentment.

'Why the sudden modesty?' Jared mocked. 'A bikini is just as revealing as your underwear.'

'Will you please leave?' It was extremely difficult to act with any dignity in the circumstances, but she managed it—just. Controlling her temper when he laughed as he casually walked from the room took conscious effort—especially when she longed to *throw* something at his departing back!

Narrawa Station was huge, even by Australian standards, with stock running into the thousands, all selectively bred and worth a fortune. The house itself was graciously old and lovingly cared for, filled with priceless antiques and period furniture. Set square on ten acres of manicured lawn and splendid gardens displaying a multitude of shrubs and native flowers, it was nothing less than a showplace, and was owned by Geoffrey Forbes, one of the Western State's wealthiest cattle barons.

Morning tea was followed two hours later by an excellent lunch, after which the men retired into the study to discuss the finer details of embryo fertilisation, leaving the women to their own devices.

'It's such a shame you have to fly back this afternoon,' said Peggy Forbes as they wandered through the gardens. 'Couldn't you stay overnight?'

Even as Kris began to demur, Louise leant forward and gave her an impulsive hug.

'Why not? We can fly back early tomorrow morning. If we left at seven it would give Alan and Jared heaps of time to get into the city.' Her face creased into a beauteous smile. 'We could take the horses out this afternoon. I bet you haven't ridden in ages. Oh, come on, Kris, say yes!'

'It's not up to me,' Kris protested. 'You'll have to ask Jared.'

Nothing would stop Louise from ascertaining an affirmative right there and then, whirling back to the house to emerge less than five minutes later wearing an ecstatic grin.

'He says it's okay. Isn't that great?'

Kris attempted to match her enthusiasm. Terrific. You'll have to lend me some clothes.' She looked down at her pale pink slacks and gave a rueful smile. 'I didn't come prepared.'

'We're the same size, and Mum still has a wardrobe full of my gear, so there's no problem.'

And there wasn't, for Louise's jeans fitted Kris perfectly, although after riding for more than an hour she wasn't sure how long she could last. Muscles she'd forgotten she had began to strain against the unaccustomed exercise, and her headache had returned with a vengeance. Jared appeared perfectly at ease on horseback, and in borrowed Levis and a bush shirt he looked the antithesis of a city-bred corporate executive.

It was after five when they brought the horses to a halt outside the stables and dismounted.

'Time for a nice leisurely shower, followed by a few drinks before dinner,' declared Louise as they walked up to the house. 'I'll check which room Mum has put you in. It's probably the East Suite overlooking the pool.'

Suite? Surely she'd misheard, Kris decided minutes later as she followed Louise upstairs. Jared and Alan were close behind, making it impossible to ask, and her faint feelings of unease rapidly gave way to consternation on discovering she was to share a room with Jared—what was more, that there was only one bed. Granted it was almost as wide as it was long, but how on earth could she dispute it without sounding positively—Victorian?

'Do you want to take the bathroom first, or shall I?'

Kris slowly lifted her head and met his enigmatic gaze. 'I don't suppose there's any way we can change this——' she swept her arm towards the bed in a gesture of pent-up anger.

'What do you have in mind?' Jared queried dryly. 'There's no urgency to get back to Perth tonight, and any excuse to do so would immediately seem contrived.'

'I'm not sleeping with you.' She endeavoured to sound calm, but there was too much resentment apparent and her voice emerged with husky vehemence.

'As long as we both *sleep*, there won't be a problem.'

His wry cynicism was more than she could bear. 'I suppose you regard this as a——'

'If I'd wanted to make love to you, I'd have instigated a seduction last night,' he interrupted hardily, and his eyes were dark with an indefinable emotion.

The fact that he could have, easily, only served to intensify her anger, although most of it was directed against herself.

'Why didn't you?' For a moment she thought she'd gone too far, and she flinched visibly as he lifted a hand to capture her chin.

'I wouldn't question my motives, if I were you,' he drawled. 'Your bargaining position is tenuous, to say the least.'

The desire to taunt him was almost impossible to ignore, and after a few electrifying minutes Kris lowered her lashes in a gesture of mute defeat. What was wrong with her, for heaven's sake? She seemed possessed of some contrary imp intent on pushing her down a path to self-destruction.

His breath fanned her face, and in seemingly slow motion she let her lashes flicker wide, her eyes solemn and unblinking as she met his dark inscrutable gaze. There was anger evident in the tight set of his jaw, an inflexibility that boded ill if she dared to pursue a course of childish truculence.

Without saying a word he pulled her close against his hardened frame, his arms resembling bands of steel from which there was no escape, then he slowly lowered his head and took possession of her mouth, parting it without any effort at all to sear the delicate inner moistness in a kiss that became nothing less than a violation of her senses.

It seemed to go on for ever, with almost brutal punishing force, and she was quite certain her ribs would crack if he didn't soon release his hold. As for attempting to breathe, it became almost impossible, and after a while she didn't even think of struggling, she just became limp, like a rag-doll, until he finally pushed her away with a husky oath of disgust.

She could only look at him wordlessly, her mouth swollen and painful from where his teeth, hers, had grazed and split the soft tissue, and she could taste the saltiness of her own blood.

His eyes raked her pale features with something akin to pitiless regard, and her hand shook slightly as she lifted it to her lips.

She felt incredibly vulnerable, as if she was teetering on the brink of some dark abyss where one false step would send her tumbling into oblivion.

With a sense of numbed fascination she watched as he caught up a change of clothes from the selection placed in the nearby wardrobe, then without a word he strode into the bathroom and within seconds she heard the muted hiss of the shower.

Kris felt totally enervated, and she held back the tears that welled and threatened to spill, stilling them by sheer willpower. She wouldn't cry, dammit, she *wouldn't*.

With an almost clinical indifference she moved towards the wardrobe and selected a dress at random, then she collected briefs, and the instant Jared entered the room she moved past him into the bathroom and closed the door.

Fifteen minutes later she was ready, her hair brushed until it resembled spun silk, her make-up skilfully perfected to hide the paleness of her features and disguise the fullness of her lips.

Jared subjected her to a brief hard glance, then he moved out of the room to pause on the landing as she joined him, and together they descended the long curving staircase to the lower floor.

Dinner was served at seven, and comprised three courses, each a pleasing complement to a well-planned combination of home-cured beef and garden-fresh vegetables, all cooked to perfection, although Kris could have forked sawdust into her mouth and her tastebuds wouldn't have known the difference.

Conversation flowed easily, and afterwards they took coffee in the lounge, sharing the companionable conviviality of several years' friendship.

Throughout it all Jared projected latent charm. The perfect guest, Kris conceded silently; a model fiancé, displaying sufficient warmth to convince the most critical observer that his affection was genuine.

It was as if they were actors on a stage playing at life by portraying an image.

The headache that had been little more than a niggle since late afternoon began to intensify, manifesting itself into a deep throbbing ache, clouding her eyes with pain.

'Kris, you've become awfully pale. Are you okay?' Louise enquired with concern, and at once all eyes swivelled towards Kris, who felt obliged to reveal the cause.

'If I could have some aspirin,' she began, deliberately avoiding Jared's piercing regard.

'It's after eleven,' Jared declared with seeming regret, standing to his feet in one fluid movement. 'Perhaps we should call it a night. We have to make an early start tomorrow.'

'Yes, of course,' Peggy Forbes agreed at once. 'I'll get some aspirin from the medicine cabinet.'

Kris almost sagged with relief at the thought of bringing the evening to an end, although several minutes later she wasn't so sure. In her anxiety to escape she had temporarily forgotten that Jared was assigned to the same room—worse, the same bed.

'It's large enough for both of us with ample space to spare,' drawled Jared within seconds of closing the door to their suite.

Kris didn't trust herself to comment, and collecting the slither of silk that Louise called a nightgown she headed for the adjoining bathroom.

She should never have come to Perth in the first place, she muttered vengefully as she discarded her clothes. Sharing the same hotel suite with Jared was bad enough, but here it was a thousand times worse. The thought of slipping between the sheets and having him lie within touching distance was sufficient to set her nerves fluttering into renewed life, making her movements jerky as she resolutely removed her make-up, then sluiced cold water over her face.

It took considerable effort to open the door and walk calmly back into the bedroom trying to look composed, when every nerve-end jangled in discordant confusion.

Jared was sitting propped against the pillows, and she felt a *frisson* of shock slip down the length of her spine at the sight of so much muscular bare flesh. Fixing her gaze on a point somewhere above his left shoulder, she said steadily,

'I've finished with the bathroom if you want to use it.'

His drawled response was a dry monosyllabic acknowledgment, but he made no move to vacate the bed, and Kris had little choice other than to slide in beside him.

'How's the headache?'

She carefully pulled the sheet up to her neck and let her head sink down on to the pillow. 'Still there.' She felt shaky and infinitely fragile, rather like a frightened lamb suddenly confronted by a prowling tiger and unsure whether she'd be permitted to escape or devoured in a bloody battle.

'If I offer my services as a masseur, you'll doubtless refuse,' he told her with weary cynicism, and she stifled a strangled reply only to hear him bid a mocking 'good night' before extinguishing the bedlamp and easing his length down the bed.

Kris felt every muscle in her body go rigid with fear. If he touched her she'd resist and fight him to her very last breath!

The seconds ticked away and became minutes as she sensed his breathing assume a regular pattern, then she nearly died as he reached out and pulled her into the curve of his body and cradled her head against one warm muscular shoulder.

'Shut up,' he admonished huskily. 'Just lie still and be quiet.'

She felt the breath choke in her throat, and every single muscle became rigid with shock. A hundred differing sensations sprang into instant life, reverberating through her body until she began to shake uncontrollably, and she was powerless to resist as he gathered her close.

A powerful leg trapped both her own, and she was frighteningly aware of its hair-roughened length, the feel of his hand as it slipped down the length of her spine, shaping her body while his lips brushed across her forehead, then trailed down to seek her mouth, grazing the tender fullness with such gentle warmth that she gradually became consumed by a treacherous weakness, an ambivalence that had everything to do with the senses.

Unconsciously she began to relax, and his hands stilled, his lips lingering for a few heartstopping seconds at the edge of her mouth, then they moved slowly up to rest at her temple.

His fingers threaded themselves through her hair in a gently soothing action, and her stomach executed a flip in slow motion as he moved his other hand and traversed the curve of her hip to settle over her breast, cupping it lightly, but clearly staking possession, slipping between the silky material with easy familiarity.

She could feel the steady beat of his heart beneath her cheek, strong and infinitely reassuring, steady, when she knew her own to be tripping at a greatly increased rate.

Would he make love to her? Somehow she didn't think so, at least not here, now. Not unless she took the next step and she wasn't sure she possessed that sort of courage. She was so close, yet in a way so far away. And Jared knew. Was it yet another calculated move on his part, this deliberate pacing in the awakening of her sensuality? Increasing her awareness, creating a maelstrom of such tumultuous magnitude that when he finally did effect a consummation she would be so emotionally attuned to him there would be no room for hesitation?

Slowly she closed her eyes, unwilling to pursue such an evocative train of thought any more. Suddenly she felt tired, and she must have drifted off to sleep at some stage, for she woke to the touch on her shoulder and discovered Jared standing beside the bed, the room filled with an early dawn light.

'Breakfast will be ready in ten minutes.'

Kris blinked, her eyes widening as she recognised her surroundings, then a delicate blush crept over her cheeks as she realised the revealing cut of her borrowed nightgown and she hurriedly pulled the covering sheet up to her shoulders in a defensive gesture which merely served to amuse him.

'Headache gone?'

Amazingly it had, and she said so, incurring his dark analytical appraisal for a few scant seconds. He seemed so remote—*detached*, she amended. In all the years she'd known him, she had yet to see him lose his temper.

'I'll wait for you downstairs.'

The instant he left the room she flung aside the sheet, took a record quick shower, changed into her clothes, then stripped the sheets from the bed and replaced the quilted coverlet. Hastily checking her watch, she flew back into the bathroom and applied moisturiser, followed it with tinted foundation, added colour to her lips, then stroked a brush through her hair. There, that would have to do.

Collecting her shoulder bag from the bedroom pedestal, she hurried from the room and ran lightly down the stairs to join Louise and her parents in the family dining-room adjoining the spacious kitchen.

'There's bacon and eggs if you want them, toast, coffee,' Peggy Forbes told her. 'Alan and Jared have already had theirs. They're making a last-minute check of the plane.'

'Toast and coffee will be fine.' Kris pulled out a chair and spread honey on to a piece of toast. 'It was kind of you to suggest we stay over.'

'Our pleasure, my dear. I don't need to say how delighted we are that you're marrying Jared.' Peggy's kindly brown eyes glowed with sincerity. 'You're perfect for one another.'

Kris almost choked on her coffee and swallowed quickly in an attempt to disguise it, feeling immensely relieved when the meal was over and they could make their way to the station wagon parked out in front ready to take them to the airstrip.

The plane stood waiting, a sleek silver jet, and after bidding Louise's parents goodbye they quickly boarded, to become airborne within minutes of taking their seats.

CHAPTER TEN

THE short flight was smooth and uneventful, and it was almost eight when Alan deposited Jared and Kris at the entrance to their hotel. Kris lifted her hand in silent farewell as the car eased into the mainstream of city traffic, then she turned and walked into the foyer.

'Care to come along to his morning's meeting?' Jared drawled as the elevator bore them swiftly upwards. 'You might find it interesting.'

Kris met his gaze and held it, trying to determine his mood. 'Won't I be in the way?'

They reached their designated floor and Jared didn't respond until they were in their suite.

'If I thought you'd be a detracting influence, I wouldn't have made the suggestion,' he replied drily.

She was filled with a curious fascination to see him in action, to witness for herself his entrepreneurial skill. 'All right,' she agreed evenly, her mind leaping to the clothes hanging in the capacious wardrobe in her room. The white Zampatti would be perfect with its sophisticated lines—thank heavens she'd packed it on a last-minute whim!

He glanced at his watch. 'Ten minutes. Can you be ready?'

She caught his look of faint scepticism, and fielded it with calm assurance. 'Of course.'

She made it with twelve seconds to spare, emerging into the lounge as Jared left his bedroom, and her eyes sparkled with merciless humour as she quickly effected a gracious

160

pirouette.

'Hm,' he considered mockingly. 'Very much the young female executive.' He picked up the key to the suite and pocketed it, then collected his briefcase and walked towards the door. 'Let's go, shall we?'

A taxi summoned by the hotel porter whisked them across half a dozen city blocks, then slid to a halt outside an imposing glass and steel structure whose white marble foyer reflected an imaginative design.

'You're going to take me in there—cold turkey?' asked Kris as they rode the elevator to the seventh floor.

He threw her a penetrating glance. 'I'm attempting to negotiate a takeover of a subsidiary company affiliated to a major Asian consortium. If I'm successful it will be a significant coup for Chayse-Laurensen; our electronics stock will soar, due to providing a necesssary edge on a very competitive market.'

They stepped out into the lushly-carpeted hallway and Kris paused slightly, her expression pensive. 'Naturally we have already acquired a number of other subsidiary companies linked to the parent consortium, and this particular deal is crucial, because it will gain us a controlling percentage.'

'Ah—you're not just a pretty face,' Jared commented, and she managed a sweet smile in response, glad to be spared the necessity of replying as they reached reception.

Within minutes they were escorted into an executive suite and introductions were effected through an interpreter, then the painstaking process of negotiations commenced in a very slow and intensely courteous manner.

Kris found it a fascinating experience, for as a spectator she shouldered none of the responsibility. It became apparent that the representative of the parent consortium intended that Jared should have no easy victory, and Kris could only applaud Jared's supreme patience in the face of his opponent's deliberate tactics.

They broke up at midday for a two-hour recess, and patronised a nearby restaurant for lunch during which Kris remained contemplatively silent.

'I thought you'd have a dozen questions—at least,' Jared remarked as he cut into a succulent looking fillet of beef.

'What would happen if you began a calculated retreat?' she ventured pensively, watching idly as he lifted his glass and took an appreciative sip of wine.

'It would be assumed I had made my highest offer, the meeting would be politely terminated—*finis*.'

'But it's a game,' she protested, and glimpsed his wry smile.

'So it is. But I must play by his rules—for now.'

'Then you intend to win?'

'I want that controlling percentage.'

'And you always get what you want,' she essayed, aware she was merely stating a fact.

'What if you fail?' It was an idle query, for she had never known Jared to fail in anything!

'I'm not foolish enough to believe I'm infallible.' His shoulders lifted in a faint shrugging gesture.

'I can't imagine you having any weaknesses. It doesn't fit in with your character.'

He pushed his plate away and sat back in his chair to regard her thoughtfully. 'Which is?'

She looked at him carefully, then ventured slowly, 'You've been part of my life for as long as

I can remember, yet there are times when I think I hardly know you.'

He considered her words with musing deliberation, then signalled for the waiter. 'Drink your wine,' he bade quietly. 'I'll order coffee, then we'd better get back.'

'That's called evading the issue.'

'This is not exactly the time or place to pursue it.'

Once again he was calling the shots, and it rankled. 'I think I'll give this afternoon a miss,' she declared, meeting his narrowed gaze with equanimity. 'I'm sure you can do without me.' The waiter arrived with their coffee, and Kris added cream and sugar, then sipped it slowly. 'I'll indulge myself with a facial and a manicure, then have my hair done.' She managed a beautiful smile. 'Then I'll go back to the hotel and relax.'

He made no attempt to dissuade her, merely paid the bill and put her into a taxi with instructions to enjoy her afternoon.

Which she did without any compunction whatsoever, arriving at the hotel shortly after five to find the suite empty. An hour later she selected a Trent Nathan dress in cream shot-silk from its hanger and slid it over her head, then she crossed to the dressing-table to attend to her make-up.

Kris heard Jared's key in the door just as she was about to stroke gloss over her lipstick, and she completed the task before moving out into the lounge.

'Were you able to make any progress with the negotiations?' she queried lightly, glimpsing his wry grimace as he dropped his briefcase and loosened his tie.

'Against the face of Asian inscrutability, it's almost impossible to categorise an answer.' He undid the top two buttons of his shirt and shrugged out of his jacket. Crossing to the bar-fridge he extracted a frosty glass, dropped in ice-cubes, added a generous measure of Bourbon and topped it with a splash of soda. 'Will you join me?'

He looked dynamic and infinitely dangerous, remotely aggressive with impatience tightly leashed and in control.

'Just fruit juice, or Perrier. Nothing alcoholic.'

Jared removed another glass, filled it, then handed it to her. 'You look exceedingly glamorous.' His eyes raked her slender frame from top to toe, then slid back to rest on her shining mouth.

Kris felt her heart give a tiny jolt, and the pulse at the base of her throat set up an erratic tattoo. 'Thank you.'

'So polite!' he mocked, swirling the contents of his glass so the ice chinked in the dark amber liquid. 'I won't be able to fly back to Sydney with you, I'm afraid. Yashuto wants another meeting tomorrow, followed by a summit in Melbourne with Loh.'

'Then you must be close to an agreement,' she said slowly.

'Perhaps.'

'How long do you think it will take?'

'If it isn't settled by Thursday, I'll withdraw my bid.' He looked ruthless and totally inflexible. 'Everything has a price—to go beyond it would reduce viability.' He lifted the glass to his mouth and swallowed half the contents in one long draught. 'I needed that.' Replacing the glass on a nearby table, he hooked his jacket over one shoulder and excused himself on the pretext of having to shower and shave, then change into an evening suit.

Louise and Alan were waiting for them in the

restaurant bar when Kris and Jared arrived, and after enjoying a drink they moved to their table.

There was an excellent band, followed by a floor show, and Kris was halfway through dessert when a familiar voice intruded with sickening clarity.

'Jared—*Kris*! Whatever are *you* doing here?' A seductive chuckle accompanied the words, and her eyes were strangely taunting. 'Such a long way from home.'

'Hello, Pamela,' Kris acknowledged evenly. 'I could ask you the same thing.'

'A modelling assignment, what else?' the svelte raven-haired beauty dismissed. 'Louise, Alan.' Her smile was brilliant as she switched her attention to Alan. 'I always mean to call whenever I'm this side of the continent, but you know how it is.'

Kris had a good idea. The tall model changed men as often as she changed her clothes, discarding one after the other with uncaring unconcern—except for Jared. Possibly because he'd discarded her, and now that he was about to be married, Pamela obviously saw him as even more of a challenge than ever. At least that was what Kris tried to tell herself.

'Won't you join us?'

Alan received a vicious jab in the ankle from Louise for his unwitting display of good manners, and although he obviously wished he could retract the invitation it was far too late, for Pamela and her escort were already ensconced, with the waiter arranging two extra chairs.

It wasn't exactly a fiasco, Kris concluded after suffering more than an hour of Pamela's superficial charm. To any observers they must appear a convivial group. Certainly the men seemed to enjoy themselves, and Pamela presided like the queen bee among her minions.

At eleven Jared called for the bill and settled it, then declared an intention to leave. Louise and Alan swiftly acceded, and Pamela reluctantly released them amid a show of affection that was markedly more explicit when it came to farewelling Jared. Granted *she* kissed him, and in public Jared had little recourse but to move out of her grasp with as much speed as politeness allowed, but the incident rankled during the short drive back to their hotel, and as soon as Alan's car was out of sight Kris lapsed into silence.

If she said one word it would release a veritable floodgate of invective, and once started, she'd never stop.

The elevator doors slid open the instant Jared pressed the call-button, and within a matter of seconds they were delivered to their floor.

Inside the suite Kris moved straight through the lounge to her bedroom and was about to enter it when a hand closed over her arm.

'Don't touch me!'

Jared turned her towards him with effortless ease. 'If you're going to take such exception to every woman I talk to——'

'*Talk?*' she snapped furiously. 'She kissed you!'

'I'm pleased you took note of that subtle distinction.'

'Don't be facetious!'

'Jealous, Kris?'

'Who said I was jealous? You only get jealous when you care, and I don't.'

His eyes assumed a watchfulness. 'Stop it,' he ordered silkily. 'You're strung up——'

'Don't you tell me what I am!' she spat out, her whole body alive with pent-up anger.

'If only Mademoiselle Jacqueline could see you now!'

He was *amused*! Somehow she could have borne anything else, even anger, but for him to resort to silent laughter was too much. Without thought her hand swung in an upward arc to land with a resounding crack against the side of his face.

For a moment she couldn't believe she'd hit him, and she stood in shocked silence, aghast, and barely registering the clenched muscle at the edge of his jaw, seeing only the red mark on his face where her hand had connected.

'Does that make you feel better?'

It made her feel terrible, but she had no intention of telling him that. 'You shouldn't have laughed.'

'It was either that, or slap you,' he retorted deliberately.

'So—*hit* me,' Kris challenged stormily as angry tears filled her eyes. 'Do it. Go on, damn you— *fight*!' Her hands balled into fists and she lashed out at him, pummelling his hard chest wherever she could strike until strong hands stilled her flailing fists, holding them fast with galling ease.

'Quit while you're ahead, Kris.'

She was too angry to take heed. 'And if I don't?'

Jared directed her a long hard glance. 'I'll give you a lesson you'll never forget.'

She gave a silent cry of pain as his hands slid up to fasten over her shoulders in a bruising grip, and her eyes assumed a fiery brilliance.

'Do you have any idea what form of retribution you could provoke?' he drawled in a dangerously quiet voice. His eyes narrowed fractionally, and she sensed the latent anger lying dormant beneath the surface of his control. *'Do you?'*

'I'm not a *child*!' she snapped resentfully.

'So you keep reminding me.'

'You could have avoided Pamela when she

simpered up to you and played kissy-face in front of everyone!'

His gaze speared her mercilessly. 'Hasn't it occurred to you that Pamela's action might be a deliberate ploy in order to create this very scene?'

'Oh—go to hell!'

'You'd try the patience of a saint,' Jared declared hardily, and her faint laugh sounded slightly off-key.

'Whereas you have a reputation for being exactly the opposite!'

It seemed an age before he spoke, and Kris shivered at the icy rage evident beneath the silkiness of his voice. 'You require proof, Kris? Is that what all this is about?'

For a few fateful seconds they seemed locked in silent battle, then Kris almost cried out as his mouth descended to crush hers, bruising in its intensity as he forced her lips apart.

She'd wanted some positive reaction, but not this—this brutal onslaught. It seemed to go on for ever, becoming a ravaging possession that destroyed every conception of what she knew a kiss to be. Her jaw ached, and her mouth felt swollen and strangely numb. Even her ribs hurt beneath the steel-like grasp of his arm as he locked her slim frame hard against his own.

She was barely able to breathe, let alone move, and just as she thought she might slip into a merciful black void her mouth was relinquished, and she drew in great gulps of air in an effort to regain her breath.

For a moment she stood swaying, then she gave an anguished moan as an arm slid beneath her knees and he lifted her high against his chest to carry her effortlessly across the room.

In the bedroom he let her slide slowly down

until her feet touched the floor, then he removed his jacket and dropped it over a nearby chair. Next came his shirt, and when his hands went to unfasten his belt the dawning realisation of what he intended was enough to freeze the blood in her veins.

'No!' The word left her lips as a scandalised whisper and her eyes flew to his, seeing the dark implacability evident, the determined resolve, and every nerve in her body shrieked with shock. 'Don't——'

'It's a little too late to beg.' He covered the short distance between them and captured her head between his hands, then he bent down and kissed her.

This time there was no anger apparent, just a wealth of seduction, almost a teasing supplication as he gently traced the outline of her lips, savouring the soft swollen fullness as they trembled slightly beneath his touch.

She wanted to cry, but no tears would come, and she let her lashes flutter down to shield the desolation mirrored in the shadowy depths of her eyes.

There was a faint slithering sound as his fingers freed the zip of her dress, and as it fell to the carpeted floor he reached for the hooks on her bra, releasing her breasts from the confining scrap of lace.

With deliberately feather-lightness he trailed his fingers over the soft contours of her breasts, shaping them with his hands, creating an evocative sensation as he succeeded in arousing each separate nerve-end until she moaned an entreaty for him to stop. Not content, he lowered his mouth to her breast to tease and tantalise one burgeoning peak before crossing to render a similar assault on the other.

Her whole body seemed to pulsate with molten fire, and she became mindless, lost in a world of sensuality so intense there was no room for anything but the need to slake the steadily swirling vortex of emotion into which she'd been drawn.

Her arms lifted to encircle his neck, holding fast his head as she exulted in a wealth of sensation, and she made no demur as he removed every last vestige of her clothing, *his*, then drew her down on to the bed. Nothing else mattered as he deliberately sought to awaken a tumultuous response, and steadily she began to scale new heights of ecstasy, discovering a degree of heightened arousal she had never imagined possible. Just as she thought she could stand no more, his mouth covered hers, stifling the agonised cry that rose in her throat as he gained entry, his throbbing manhood an alien hurtful force as it thrust towards her central core.

She surfaced through a threshold of pain, clutching his shoulders, pushing at them in an effort to be free of him, whimpering in frightened disbelief as she attempted to tear her mouth away from his own.

Jared paused, gentling her wildly threshing body, then slowly he began to move, pacing gently until pleasure gradually overtook pain, creating a deep throbbing ache that soon spiralled out of control, absorbing her completely in his deep rhythmic possession.

It seemed an age before she lay spent and dreamily exhausted at his side, curled lightly against his muscular length.

She must have dozed, for when she woke it was still dark, and moving cautiously she slid from the bed and made her way to the bathroom. Ignoring the shower, she filled the spa, added scented oil, then stepped into the pulsating water and sank down, letting it cleanse and soothe until she felt deliciously drowsy. Emerging, she reached for a towel and wound it sarong-wise round her slim curves, then she attended to her toilette, caught up a dark silk robe and donned it before making her way out to the lounge.

She felt inordinately thirsty, and crossing to the bar-fridge she poured herself a glass of chilled water, drank it, and moved towards the window. Instead of being tired, she felt curiously alive, and not in the least inclined to retreat back to bed and sleep.

Kris stood looking out over the city, watching the flickering images of various coloured neon signs against the moonlit skyline, then her attention wandered and relived again the events leading up to her explosive argument with Jared and its stormy aftermath.

In retrospect she was forced to deal with a whole gamut of emotions, not the least being a degree of shame for losing her temper. As for hitting him—she'd never hit anyone before in her life!

A slight sound alerted her, and she turned to see Jared's tall frame silhouetted against the room's darkness as he crossed to stand behind her.

'Unable to sleep?'

She swallowed convulsively, feeling acutely vulnerable and shy. 'I didn't mean to disturb you,' she murmured, and sensed his faint smile as he lifted a hand and threaded his fingers through her hair, then he caught hold of her shoulders and pulled her back against him.

A shaft of exquisite pleasure exploded deep inside as his lips settled against the delicate curve of her neck, his tongue an erotic instrument as he traced the throbbing pulse, then brushed a path across her sensitive nape.

Her body was its own traitorous mistress, brought vibrantly alive by his touch, and she closed her eyes as she allowed her senses to take over, glorying in the rapturous stimulation until a fierce hunger arose, demanding assuagement.

'Jared——' There were so many things she wanted to say, her throat ached with their suppression, and her lips parted soundlessly as he turned her into his arms and claimed her mouth in a poignantly sweet kiss.

'Come back to bed,' he husked gently.

The thought of sharing again those hitherto unexplored intimacies brought a soft flush to her cheeks, and her arms curled round his neck as he scooped her high and carried her back to his room.

The need to please and be pleasured was uppermost, and beneath his guidance her hesitant explorative touch became more bold, heightening an arousal of such agonising sweetness that she was driven half-mad, sobbing acquiescence and begging his possession as their lovemaking assumed a wild passionate quality, dissolving her inhibitions as if they had never existed.

Satiated at last, she slept, her body entwined with his, and the steady beat of his heart beneath her cheek provided security and a curious sense of peace.

CHAPTER ELEVEN

WITHIN an hour of arriving back in Sydney, Kris felt as if she'd never been away. Angela seemed hell-bent on stage-managing the social event of the year, and had successfully organised every waking hour during the ensuing few days, co-ordinating fittings, rehearsals, hair appointments—the list was endless!

Only Louise's company made it all bearable, for together they were alternately able to commiserate or laugh, or in one case cry, as Angela pushed relentlessly forward with no visible sign of wilting. There was scarcely time in which to think, let alone to dwell on anything except the wedding.

Jared phoned once, a brief call in the early dawn hours to tell her he would be arriving on Friday evening. Maddening was the fact that Kris had struggled through the mists of sleep and merely uttered monosyllabic inanities to his brisk queries, and only after replacing the receiver did she curse herself for not asking a single question, or saying the three most important words that had filled her brain during every waking hour since her return from Perth.

Friday was fraught with innumerable phone calls, and a seemingly incessant stream of people invading the house with gifts. Angela wore a permanent frown, and Suzy was the antithesis of her usual calm self.

Consequently it was something of a relief to escape to the airport in order to meet Jared's incoming flight, and Kris waited with scant

patience, her eyes searching for his endearingly
familiar head as passengers slowly filtered into the
arrival lounge.

Then he was there, and she stood hesitantly
unsure whether she should follow the dictates of
her heart and rush into his arms. He looked so
aloof, despite an inherent vitality apparent,
magnifying her awareness of him to a point where
she could scarcely find voice.

Kris clasped her hands together, unconsciously
twisting the slim circle of gold round her finger,
adjusting the large, exquisitely-cut diamond so
that it rested squarely, then she pushed her hands
out of sight behind her back, feeling about as
confident and assured as a gauche thirteen-year-
old schoolgirl.

'Hello.' It was meant to sound cool, but instead
the greeting came out as a slightly breathless
embodiment of all her pent-up emotions, and her
expression held a haunting vulnerability that lent a
strange defenceless quality to her features.

For a brief second Jared's eyes flared, darkening
with definable passion, then assumed a sardonic
gleam as he moved towards her.

'Shall we go?'

Quite what she expected, she wasn't sure. A
bruising kiss, perhaps; or, equally unsatisfactory,
the teasing brush of his lips across her own. Never
once during the past few days had she imagined
their reunion would be so—*conventional*.

The touch of his hand at her elbow, albeit
lightly, sent an electric charge through her veins,
quickening her pulse until her whole body seemed
to reverberate with the deep thudding beat of her
heart.

All the way out to the car she wore a fixed
smile, supremely conscious of his proximity, her

muscles screaming with silent tension, making her aware of every breath she took.

The Porsche stood in its reserved car space, and she silently handed him the keys, then she slid into the passenger seat and reached for the seatbelt as he snapped the door closed and crossed round to slip in behind the wheel.

Once the vehicle was clear of the airport periphery, Jared eased it into the heavy flow of traffic, negotiating the many intersections with skill as he joined the main arterial road leading towards the inner eastern suburbs.

At Double Bay he swung the sleek car into a curved street and sought to park it, eventually sliding into an empty bay adjacent to the main centre.

There were a number of eating establishments in the immediate vicinity, and Kris didn't demur as he led her towards a restaurant. When they were seated he ordered a fine Veuve Clicquot, then, when their glasses were filled, he raised his in silent salute, reaching out to touch the rim of her glass with his own before lifting it to his lips and savouring a generous quantity.

How would he react if she said *I love you*? How *could* she say it here? Yet she wanted to, just as she needed to see those unfathomable dark eyes lose their faint brooding quality, the strong jaw relax, and have his sensuously moulded mouth curve into a warm mobile smile.

There were a number of questions she wanted to ask; like where they were going for their honeymoon—not that the destination mattered, but it was important for her to know what she needed to pack. And if he wanted to be able to skip the next twenty-four hours as much as she did, to bypass completely the madness of tomorrow when publicity would ensure that their special day would be about as private as a three-ring circus. But most important of them all was—did he love her?

Tomorrow night would he do more than physically slake his desire, having sated her own with the same consummate ease he had displayed a mere few nights ago?

The perplexity of it all marred her appetite, and she scarcely did justice to the excellent *ratatouille*, merely toyed with her portion of *coq au vin*, and declined dessert, preferring to sip her wine in the hope that her stomach would behave itself for what remained of the evening.

Jared ate with evident enjoyment, adroitly filling the empty spaces in conversation with meaningless information which she barely registered, let alone retained for more than a few scant minutes.

To all outward appearances they presented an attentive bond, and Kris wondered if anyone saw beneath their amicable façade.

Jared refused coffee, and although their meal had been a leisurely one, it was barely eight o'clock when they vacated their table, and after signing the bill he led her out to the car.

Instead of turning back towards Darling Point he made his way eastward, and Kris felt her nerves tighten measurably as he drove in beneath his own apartment block.

'Come up and make me some coffee.'

His voice was deliberately bland, and Kris kept her attention focused on the brick wall beyond the windscreen. To refuse would be futile, as well as ridiculous. She had already shared his bed, and given twenty-odd hours they would be husband and wife.

'I——' she faltered, beginning to feel thoroughly wretched.

'My dear Kris,' he drawled silkily, taking the keys from the ignition, 'just get out of the car, like a good girl, will you?'

It was far easier to comply, and she walked to the elevator at his side, aware of him to a degree that was frightening. In the confined space his frame seemed much larger, his height and breadth intimidating, and although he gave the appearance of indolent ease she could sense a leashed quality, almost as if he was keeping a tight rein on his emotions.

Entering the penthouse apartment proved to be something of an anti-climax, and Kris moved towards the kitchen with a kind of desperate haste, extracting the percolator and filling the container with water before spooning ground coffee beans into the filter and setting it on a hotplate.

The need to occupy herself was paramount, and she found cups and saucers, sugar and cream, then when the coffee was ready she poured it and carried the tray into the lounge.

'Come and sit down.'

Beside him on the comfortable two-seater? It would be more than she could bear. Without a word she set the tray down, handed him a cup and its saucer, then took her own to a nearby chair.

'Afraid I might eat you?' Jared drawled, and she cast him a swift glance from beneath carefully veiled lashes.

How did she explain that she felt more afraid of him at this moment than ever before, at odds with her own emotions and terribly unsure of him? Possibly a quantum could be attributed to sheer bridal nerves, but to feel so disproportionately on edge was pure folly.

'Where is the beautiful young girl who gifted me not only her body, but the most treasured gift a man could ask of the woman he wants as his wife?' he asked softly.

Kris had to say something, if only to break the silence into which she seemed locked, and her voice came out in a choked husky whisper. 'Virginity is supposed to be an outmoded cliché.'

'Among most of your contemporaries, I'm sure that it is.'

'And yours.' The words escaped from her lips before she had a chance to stop them, and she glimpsed his wry smile.

'There will always be women who are prepared to use their charms for material gain. The practice is as old as Eve.'

'I'll have to remember that when I want you to buy me something special.' Why was she being so flippant when all she wanted was to be in his arms? It didn't make sense.

'Come here and say that.'

She felt as if she'd suddenly skated on to very thin ice, and her eyes widened with mesmerised fascination as he stood in one fluid movement. To sit where she was invited madness, yet there was nowhere to run.

'Jared——'

He dispensed with her cup and saucer with one hand while pulling her towards him with the other.

'I don't want——'

'Liar.'

His breath teased her temples, disturbing the soft tendrils of hair as he bent his head and trailed a path across her forehead with his lips, teasing, tasting their way over the delicate bones of her face, moving ever downwards until they hovered fractionally over her mouth. Not content, he traced the curved outline with the edge of his tongue, then began to probe the sweet moistness within until she gave a silent moan of entreaty, opening her mouth to him without thought of denial.

His kiss became everything she had hungered for, and more, blotting out all the insecurities, the vague anxiety she had experienced during the past few days. There was only *now*, the thud of her heart beating in rapid unison with his own as he wreaked havoc with a ravaging exploration that threatened loss of control.

Unbidden, her hands slid over the tightly-corded muscles ridging his back, feeling their sinewy tenseness beneath the smooth silk of his shirt, and she traced a pattern across the breadth of his shoulders, revelling in their strength, the hardness of his arms, before creeping up to caress the hair at his nape, loving the crisp thickness as she moulded the shape of his head, holding it as he gave an inaudible groan and let his mouth slip down to rest against the hollow at the base of her throat.

Seeking a throbbing pulse, he teased it with his tongue, then pulled it gently into his mouth, and the action created a wild surge of liquid fire, igniting her body until she became totally inflamed, wanting, *needing* so much more.

Nothing else mattered except her desire to pleasure him, to experience again those mindless myriad sensations so exquisite that the rapture almost defied description. She had so much to learn, so much she wanted to give of herself that the agonising sweetness became a tangible pain.

The fact that she could unashamedly beg his possession was something she found intensely shocking. Equally damning was her own treacherous response, the awareness that she could behave like a primitive wanton in his arms.

Even now her fingers moved of their own volition to the buttons on his shirt in the need to touch his skin, the soft springy hair matting his chest, and she uttered a tiny moan in protest as a hand covered her own, stilling the movement with obvious reluctance.

'No.' Jared caught hold of her arms and held her away, and she looked up at him in dazed silence, bewildered and bereft by his rejection.

He uttered a husky oath as his hands slid up to cradle her head, then his mouth closed over hers in a brief evocative caress, and her eyes ached with suppressed tears beneath the darkness of his gaze.

'It would be so easy to make love to you,' Jared murmured deeply, searching the stark vulnerability evident as she met his eyes. 'God knows, I want to,' he groaned emotively. 'But once in my bed, I'd never allow you to leave.' A faint deprecatory smile tugged the corners of his mouth. 'I care enough to want tomorrow to be a day you remember as being special in every way. Not beginning with a furtive return home in the early dawn hours, witnessed by servants, perhaps even Angela herself, risking censure.' He paused, and she sensed the smile in his voice by the faint quirk evident as his lips trailed towards her temple before slipping down her cheekbone to rest against the edge of her mouth. 'Humour me, hm?'

Her smile felt tremulous and infinitely shaky as she drew away from him. 'So now you take me home?'

His answering smile was incredibly wry. 'Yes. Before I lose sight of my honourable intentions.'

'Somehow I've never imagined you to be noble-minded,' Kris told him softly minutes later as the car whispered the short distance through near-empty streets, and she caught his dark gleaming glance as he turned briefly towards her.

'No? In this instance I can promise you it will be worth it.'

And it was. Starting with a beautiful cloudless sky with just the merest hint of a breeze that was a photographer's dream.

Kris wafted through the morning in a state of bemusement as Angela and Suzy ran hither and yon checking and double-checking a seemingly endless contingent of necessities, clucking like distraught hens when the floral delivery was a mere ten minutes late, the dressmaking designer's assistant arrived too early, and only two hairdressers reported in when three had been requested. Louise, together with the flowergirl and pageboy, arrived shortly after lunch, and by then Kris was inclined to believe she was the only sane one among the lot of them!

The ceremony itself bore all the overtones of a gala performance, warranting not only media attention as they emerged from the historic old church, but television coverage as well. It was, as Jared so aptly murmured in a quiet aside, strictly smile-time.

A gruelling photographic session, during which Kris wondered more than once if so many shots were necessary in an attempt to record the event for posterity, was immediately followed by a sumptuous reception in true fairytale fashion.

And if she felt ethereal attired in her wedding finery as she stood beside Jared, she put such light-headedness down to the excellent champagne she had sipped during the ensuing few hours until it was time for Sam to whisk them back to Darling Point in order to change.

Even then there was no time alone, and it wasn't

until they had returned to the reception and taken their leave in traditional manner that they finally escaped into the waiting car.

'I never thought we'd make it,' Kris ventured minutes later when Jared cleared the parking area.

A dark gleaming glance slanted towards her before he centred his attention on the road ahead. 'You looked beautiful,' he told her gently, and her heart tripped and accelerated its beat at his compliment.

'Thank you,' she acknowledged with the utmost sincerity. 'You were quite riveting yourself.'

He bypassed the city, heading west, and she leaned her head back against the cushioned rest before turning to look at him.

'Where are we going?'

He leaned forward and pushed a tape into the cassette-deck, adjusting the volume so that the sound emerged from the speakers in soft muted tones. 'Close your eyes, I'll wake you when we get there.'

To her amazement she did doze, not consciously, but the light touch on her arm roused her sufficiently to note that the car was stationary in a dimly-lit driveway.

It looked terribly familiar, and she turned slowly towards him. 'The Blue Mountains retreat?'

His smile was lazy and full of amusement. 'No phones, except the one in the car with its own answering service in case of dire emergency. No restaurants, no fellow guests. Just us.'

'No need to dress up,' added Kris, and felt her pulse leap into vibrant life at the way he was looking at her.

'I don't plan on you being dressed very much of the time.'

A delicious bubble of laughter rose up from her

hroat as she reached for the doorclasp. 'Shall we go
n?'

There wasn't a speck of dust to be seen, and
both the cupboards and refrigerator were well
tocked with sufficient food to last several weeks.

'I guess I'll have to cook.' Culinary artistry was
one of her favourite hobbies, and indulging it
vould be no hardship.

'We'll share.'

They were standing in the lounge, and she
vatched as Jared crossed to the bar, extracted a
bottle of champagne, opened it, then filled two
glasses with bubbling light golden liquid.

'To us,' Jared declared solemnly, and she lifted
her glass in silent acceptance, her eyes unconsciously flicking to the strong column of his throat as
he savoured a quantity of the champagne, noting
the strength apparent, the sheer animal magnetism
he exuded without any effort at all.

Kris let her gaze slip down to rest on the second
button of his immaculate shirt. It seemed
incredible that now they were alone she should feel
o defenceless; achingly aware of him, yet
trangely hesitant to make the slightest move. She
vanted so much to be a part of him, to become
ost in the physical mastery of his lovemaking, yet
deep down there was a terrible sadness in the
knowledge that the one intrinsic quality she most
desired would be absent.

Perhaps it was asking too much to hope love
might enter into their relationship. She was mad to
xpect that it could. How could she put into words
vhat she felt without laying bare her soul? If she was
ure of him, it would be the easiest thing in the world
o say 'I love you'. Except that too many factors had
ontributed towards this marriage.

'What's going on in that head of yours, then?'

Startled, her eyes flew wide, then fluttered dow
as she lowered her lashes in an attempt to veil he
soul against that deep penetrating gaze, and sh
swallowed compulsively as he took the glass fro
her nerveless fingers and placed it together with hi
own on a nearby table.

There was nothing she could do to escape th
firm touch of his fingers beneath her chin, lifting
so that she had little option but to look at hin
She wanted to cry out in protest against his inter
appraisal, hating the ease with which she began t
respond, tinging her skin with delicate colour a
every nerve-end seemed to tingle alive, and th
warmth deep within began to radiate until
encompassed her entire body, pulsating with
deafening beat she was sure he must hear.

Perhaps the champagne was to blame, or mayb
it was just sheer reaction to the day and all
entailed—realisation that she had arrived at th
moment around which her life had been planne
The bitter irony of it all was that she no longe
possessed any pride, the one quality she ha
thought to retain. Jared had only to touch her an
she melted, a willing supplicant for any attentio
he was prepared to bestow.

'Regrets—so soon?'

'No, of course not,' Kris responded steadil
and glimpsed his faint smile.

'I'm relieved to hear it.'

It was impossible to gauge his mood, whether h
was being genuinely solicitous or merely providin
her with the opportunity to present an excuse an
retire.

Maybe bed would be the best solution. At lea
there she could give herself up to the magic of h
lovemaking, pretend under cover of darkness tha
the elusive alchemy they shared was more tha

just mere physical need.

'It's been a long day,' she said quietly, moving away from him as he released her, and without a further word she turned and made her way down the hallway.

In the main bedroom she crossed to the window and slid it open, becoming aware of various night sounds in the still evening air. Secluded so far from the main road and surrounded by bush beyond the firebreak inevitably brought rustlings amid twigs and dry leaves as nocturnal animals sought sustenance and prowled through the undergrowth. Small furtive creatures, reptiles lying in wait for an unwary prey. In the distance there was an imperceptible glow of reflected electric lights from the nearest township, casting a pale golden light against the inky black sky.

With a sigh Kris closed the curtains, the soft swishing sound masking Jared's entry into the room, and she gave a slight start as she turned and saw him standing there.

'Our luggage.'

Of course, how could she have forgotten?

'You use this bathroom, I'll take what I need into the other one.'

Words seemed superfluous, and she merely nodded as she watched him cross to lift an overnight bag on to a nearby chair. Unzipping it, he extracted a toiletry kit, then he walked calmly from the room.

He undoubtedly had been in this situation countless times before, whereas she merely felt awkward and very much the traditional blushing bride. Except that she shouldn't feel awkward or ill at ease. A few days ago she had melted into his arms and into his bed without so much as a qualm or a vestige of guilt. Why tonight of all nights

should she suddenly develop an attack of nerves?
It hardly made sense.

Moving towards the bed, she turned back the
coverlet and plumped the pillows, then she took
what she needed from her bag and crossed to the
bathroom.

The shower soothed away some of her nervous
tension, and towelled dry, her toilette completed, she
slipped a wispy creation of nylon and lace over her
head and pulled on the matching négligé. The delicate peach tonings lent colour to her pale features,
and she pulled a wry face at her mirrored reflection
as she tugged a brush through her silvery-blonde
hair. Without make-up she looked even younger
than her twenty-one years, her eyes wide and luminous, their depths shadowed and strangely poignant.

Damn, this would never do. In a minute Jared
would come to the door and ask why she was
taking so long, perhaps even be slightly amused at
her sudden bout of shyness. Now was not the
moment to be timid.

Before she could change her mind she opened
the door and emerged into the bedroom, faltering
to a halt when she saw Jared sitting on the edge of
the bed.

For a number of heart-stopping seconds he just
looked at her, then he bade softly, 'Come here.'

The overhead light had been extinguished and
there was only the muted glow of the bedside lamp
illuminating the room. Attired in a black silk robe,
he looked vaguely satanical, and Kris felt her body
tremble at the darkness reflected in his eyes.

'I don't think I can.'

His mouth curved into a slow warm smile. 'It's
easy. You simply put one foot in front of the other.'

'Perhaps you should come and get me,' she
ventured shakily, not sure her legs would carry her.

'Do you want me to?'

I want you to hold me, she cried silently. Close. And help me make it through to the part where I lose myself in sheer feeling and not care that love has nothing to do with it.

'Please.' Was that her voice, that disembodied whisper so low and indistinct she could scarcely hear it herself?

Jared didn't move except to reach out his hand towards her, and after a minute she took a few steps forward, then she placed her hand tentatively in his, allowing him to pull her unresisting towards him.

Her legs touched his, and this close she was made frighteningly aware of his masculinity, a primeval force that was impossible to ignore.

The desire to touch him was uppermost, yet she held back, waiting, afraid of the depth of her consuming passion and even more afraid of unleashing it for fear of inviting his amusement.

He was accustomed to women skilled in the art of giving physical pleasure, not relatively untutored innocents who responded by instinct alone, craving intimacies with a degree of wanton abandonment that she had never envisaged except in her wildest dreams—or darkest nightmare. Certainly she had never imagined the sexual act could be such a total ravishment of the senses.

'I have something for you.'

Kris felt her eyes widen slightly, then the breath caught in her throat as he withdrew a slim jeweller's case from the bedside table and placed it in her hand.

She was incapable of saying so much as a word, and her fingers shook slightly as they slid open the catch. Inside, a gold heart-shaped locket nestled in its bed of silk, delicately engraved with whorls so that it resembled a precious keepsake of another era.

'Open it,' Jared directed quietly, and she slipped the two halves apart, giving a soundless gasp at the magnificent ruby surrounded totally by diamonds.

'Turn it over. There's an inscription.'

Kris traced a finger over the engraved calligraphy, her eyes welling with tears as she read, *Krista—my love, my life. My wife.*

With gentle fingers he slid the twin halves closed, then placed the delicate linked chain over her head, trailing its length to the place where the locket lay in the valley between her breasts.

A solitary tear spilled and ran down her cheek to land with a silent plop on his hand, and was immediately followed by another and yet another as a wealth of feeling welled up inside, all-consuming, exultant.

'I love you,' she whispered, lifting her hands to his face, touching the strongly etched features, tracing the sculptured outline of his jaw, his cheekbone, before lingering at the edge of his mouth. 'I always have; I always will.'

'I know.' He kissed her fingers, then teased their tips with his tongue, pulling first one then the other into his mouth before burying his lips into her palm, circling the soft skin with erotic sensitivity. Slowly he lifted his head, and she almost died at the ardent warmth evident in his gaze.

'The past five years have been hell. Waiting— becoming increasingly impatient for you to grow up. Afraid your feelings for me would change. Wanting to love you until there could be no room for anyone else to infiltrate your emotions.' A wry smile curved his generous mouth, a self-deprecatory gesture against his own vulnerability, so that she could only marvel that there had ever been a time when he was unsure of her.

Assurance gave her the confidence to bend her

head down to his, and her lips brushed across his own, trembling a little as she instigated a tentative exploration.

For a few heady minutes he allowed her licence to initiate the foray, then his hands slid up her arms to hold fast her head as he wrought a devastating assault on her senses, plundering until she clung to him, hardly aware of the tiny guttural sounds that rose and became trapped in her throat.

When he at last broke the kiss she rested limply in his arms, bemused by the force of his passion and bewitched to a degree where she could only stand looking at him in tremulous wonderment.

Gently he lowered his head, burying his mouth in the tantalising cleft between her breasts, and she felt a familiar surge of emotion consume her limbs, spiralling upwards until she was on fire.

With the utmost care he slowly removed her négligé, then gradually eased the ribbon straps of her nightgown over her shoulders.

'Jared.' His name was an almost inaudible groan as he sought one hardened roseate peak and savoured it, tantalising at leisure before trailing slowly to render a similar treatment to its twin.

He raised his head, and she almost died at the wealth of passionate desire evident, a deep slumbrous warmth that promised ecstasy.

'Dear sweet Kris,' he murmured huskily. 'I've hungered for you so long. Wanting, needing you. Will you let me love you every day of my life, to make up for all the days—*nights*, that I've missed?'

An inner radiance was responsible for the soft glow reflecting from the depths of her eyes, and without hesitation she wound her arms around his neck.

'Yes, please! Starting now,' she whispered, sure in the knowledge that enchantment, although it had had its dark moments, was theirs for a lifetime.

Harlequin Presents

Coming Next Month

Available in June wherever paperback books are sold, or through Harlequin Reader Service:

In the U.S.
901 Fuhrmann Blvd.
P.O. Box 1397
Buffalo, N.Y. 14240-1397

In Canada
P.O. Box 603
Fort Erie, Ontario
L2A 5X3

Take 4 books & a surprise gift FREE

SPECIAL LIMITED-TIME OFFER

Mail to   **Harlequin Reader Service®**

In the U.S.   In Canada
901 Fuhrmann Blvd.   P.O. Box 609
P.O. Box 1394   Fort Erie, Ontario
Buffalo, N.Y. 14240-1394   L2A 5X3

YES!   Please send me 4 free Harlequin Romance® novels and my free surprise gift. Then send me 6 brand-new novels every month as they come off the presses. Bill me at the low price of $1.66 each*—a 15% saving off the retail price. There are no shipping, handling or other hidden costs. There is no minimum number of books I must purchase. I can always return a shipment and cancel at any time. Even if I never buy another book from Harlequin, the 4 free novels and the surprise gift are mine to keep forever.   116 BPR BP7S

*$1.75 in Canada plus 69¢ postage and handling per shipment.

Name   (PLEASE PRINT)

Address   Apt. No.

City   State/Prov.   Zip/Postal Code

This offer is limited to one order per household and not valid to present subscribers. Price is subject to change.   DOR-SUB-1A

ATTRACTIVE, SPACE SAVING BOOK RACK

Display your most prized novels on this handsome and sturdy book rack. The hand-rubbed walnut finish will blend into your library decor with quiet elegance, providing a practical organizer for your favorite hard-or soft-covered books.

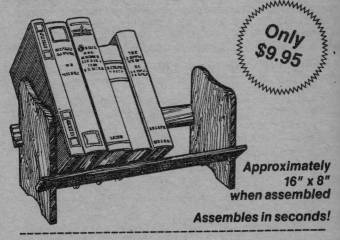

Only $9.95

Approximately 16" x 8" when assembled

Assembles in seconds!

To order, rush your name, address and zip code, along with a check or money order for $10.70* ($9.95 plus 75¢ postage and handling) payable to *Harlequin Reader Service*:

Harlequin Reader Service
Book Rack Offer
901 Fuhrmann Blvd.
P.O. Box 1325
Buffalo, NY 14269-1325

Offer not available in Canada.

*New York residents add appropriate sales tax.

BKR-1R